Late Decisions

IVY MARIE

Ivy
Marie

IVY MARIE PUBLISHING

Contents

Prologue One

LEXI

I LOOKED AT THE picture of the man I was supposed to be meeting again. I don't know how many times I looked at it, but by now, I had it memorized. He was average-looking, with brown hair, brown eyes and a polite smile. Nothing about him stood out. We both swiped right, matching us on a dating app. We've been talking for a few weeks before we set up this in-person date.

I opened the app to see if he'd sent me a message. Nothing. It's already been half an hour. I was debating on messaging him when a text from my best friend, Roxanne, came in.

Rox: How's the date?

> **Me:** He didn't show.

> **Rox:** Jerk. I'm sorry. Want to come over?

> **Me:** Thanks, but I think I'll just go home. Besides, you have the grand opening tomorrow.

> **Rox:** Lexi.

> **Me:** You don't need to worry about me. I'll be fine.

> **Rox:** We'll talk tomorrow. Don't comatose yourself with ice cream.

> **Me:** No promises.

For the first time in my life, I was stood up. Trying to find 'the one' is going to be a lot harder than I'd hoped. Rox's parents found each other, and that's been it for them. That's what I want. Is that so hard? *Maybe I should lower my expectations.*

Five more minutes, then I'll leave. Two men walked into the bar. One has brown hair, and the other has dirty blond hair. Neither one of them was my date. My shoulders slumped as I watched them over my glass of vodka cranberry. They ordered a beer at the bar and then went to sit at a booth.

If my date wasn't going to show, then maybe I should pick someone up for the night. Past dates were more interested in sweet-talking me into bed than getting to know me. I've consistently turned them down, but it's been a long time. *One night of fun, then I'll resume my search.*

"Hi."

A sexy rumble of a male voice sent chills of pleasure rolling down my spine. I looked over to see the blond from a few minutes ago. He stood behind the empty bar stool next to me, his beer bottle held loosely in his hand as he stared down at me.

"Hi." I said a little breathless.

"What's a beautiful woman like you doing drinking alone? Especially in this place?"

"Actually, I was on my way out."

"That's too bad." He frowned. "I would have loved to join you."

"What about your friend?" I jerked my chin in the direction of the booth. "The brown-haired man you walked in with?"

His lips quirked upward, and there was a sparkle of amusement in his eyes. "So, you noticed me walk in, huh?"

"Maybe." I elongated the word.

"Well?" He gestured to the empty bar stool. "Would you like my company for the evening?"

I bit my lip, contemplating his offer. *He could be fun in bed.* The man is handsome, from his green eyes to his broad shoulders to his waist. My gaze froze on the badge and gun at his waist.

"You're a cop?"

He looked down at the badge. "Detective, actually."

"Oh."

Images of being handcuffed to the bed floating in my head. Surprising me on how arousing I found it.

"Does it bother you?" He took a half step back.

I smiled, looking back up at him through my lashes. "Not at all."

"Then, may I join you for a drink?"

I gestured to the seat next to me. "My name is Lexi."

"Tyler." He signalled for the bartender as he took the seat. "What will be your poison? Another cocktail?"

"Beer. I'll take a blond on tap."

Tyler grinned, then turned to the bartender. "Two beers, one blond and one lager, both on tap. I'll add her previous drink onto my tab."

"Sure thing, detective." The bartender poured our drinks and then placed them down on the counter. "Enjoy."

"So, Lexi, why are you drinking alone?" Tyler prodded.

"I got stood up."

He frowned. "What kind of jerk would neglect a woman?"

I shrugged. "Tonight was the first time we were going to meet."

"Blind date?"

"Sort of. We've been chatting on a dating app for a while before planning this night."

Tyler scowled. His reaction caused a flutter in my stomach. I couldn't help but smile. It made me happy that he was disgusted on my behalf. At least, that's how I interpreted his scowl.

"What?" I asked curiously.

"Two things." He began. "No man is worth your time if he never showed up for a planned date. And secondly, I'm not a fan of dating apps."

"Why not?"

"I don't believe a real connection can be made through those apps."

"So, you're a romantic?" I teased.

"Not exactly." Tyler smiled. "My parents met through work and have been together since. It's because of them that I believe that there is someone out there for me, and I won't be meeting her through a dating app."

My eyes widened. Both his smile and his words caught me off guard. Tyler's green eyes sparkled with amusement as he looked at me. It made my stomach flutter. It's a strange feeling, something that I've never experienced before. Being with Tyler, despite only just meeting him, feels natural. He believes in 'the one' like I do. *Could he be it for me?*

"It's getting late, Lexi." Tyler announced after a couple of hours of talking. "Should I escort you home?"

"Or, you could take me home." I flirted, batting my eyes and hoping I wasn't reading the signs wrong.

His eyes darkened with lust. "It would be my pleasure."

Tyler paid for his tab, then took my hand and led me outside. The electric spark from his touch nearly had me on my knees. It was so strong. I've felt the tingle of a spark before, which led to a second date, but nothing like this. The anticipation for what was to come when we got to his place put a smile on my face as I leaned into him while we walked.

Tyler stopped at the parking lot behind the bar. "Um, did you drive here?"

"I did."

"Then I'll drive your car to my house. Mine is still at the station."

A giggle slipped out as I handed him my car keys. "Why would you do that?"

"The plan was for my partner to take me back to collect it after we had a couple of beers to unwind from the day." He grinned. "Then I saw you at the bar, and my priorities shifted."

"So the man you came in with is your partner?"

"He is." His smile broadened. "I love that you watched me enter."

"I was looking for my date." I tugged him toward my car. "This is me."

Tyler unlocked the car and opened my door. Then he went over to the driver's side and adjusted the seat and mirrors before backing up and pulling onto the road. I kept my phone in my hand, ready to dial Roxanne if I was wrong about this man and was actually being lured to my death. There are too many stories online and on TV about dates going horribly wrong. He kept my hand in his as he drove, slightly above the speed limit, through the streets of Frostham.

His thumb rubbed rhythmically over the back of my hand, slowly building my arousal. Butterflies fluttered in my gut when Tyler slowed down in a peaceful-looking neighbourhood. I feel the same sense of excitement right now as I do when I am settled into the seat for a roller coaster.

"Home sweet home." Tyler said, parking the car and getting out.

I got out of the car before he could come around to open the door and looked up at the house. It was the end unit of a fourplex. *A detective must make a decent salary.* I could never afford a house. I'm still renting an apartment. Tyler handed me my car keys, then tugged me up the front steps, unlocked his house, and then pulled me inside. He locked the door, turned on a light, then cupped my face and kissed me. I barely had time to put my purse down before he captured my lips.

"I've been wanting to do that all night." He admitted.

Tyler leaned back in, his lips taking possession of mine. Instantly, I parted for him, and Tyler took full advantage. His tongue swept into my mouth, exploring, teasing, and deepening the kiss. My fingers balled into his shirt, holding on for dear life as my mind went fuzzy.

There was a bark, and Tyler pulled back with a groan. "I have a dog."

"So I heard." I smiled at him. "Are you going to introduce us?"

"Lexi, this is Lucky." Tyler stepped back and gestured to a beagle. "He's a rescue dog, abused by his previous owner, so don't feel bad if he doesn't take a shine to you."

Slowly, I went to my knees and held out a hand. "Hi, Lucky."

The beagle didn't move from his spot a safe distance away. I stayed on the ground a moment longer, waiting, then he moved. Cautiously, he sniffed my hand. Lucky looked up at me as if he was trying to decide what to make of me. Then he moved closer, planted his front paws on my knees and barked at me. With a laugh, I petted his head, and Lucky's tail wagged.

"Wow." Tyler said, awe clear in his tone. "I've never seen him take to someone as quickly as he did with you."

"It must be a sign." I teased.

"Must be." He agreed.

I looked up at Tyler. He was watching me with those lust-filled green eyes, but there was something else there — something I couldn't identify. Tyler picked up the beagle, held him like a baby, and scratched at his belly.

"Okay, bud, that's enough." He set the dog down and helped me up. "I want Lexi all to myself."

Heat rose to my cheeks. Tyler guided me upstairs to his bedroom and closed the door. Pressing me into it, he kissed me again. He was not as needy as he was at the front door, but he was just as possessive. My arms wrapped around his neck. Tyler skimmed his hands down my sides to my waist.

"Too many clothes." He growled.

"Yes." I agreed.

Together, we worked on removing each other's clothes while still kissing and walking closer to the bed. It was a skill that I've only read about in books. The back of my legs hit the bed. Without missing a beat, Tyler lifted me and placed me on the mattress. His lips left mine to trail kisses down my neck and across my collarbone. Reaching behind me, he unhooked my bra and pulled the material away.

"Tyler!" I moaned, back arching off the bed when his mouth clamped around my breast.

His hand was on my other breast, messaging and tweaking the nipple while his mouth sucked and nibbled the other nipple. I moaned, my breathing becoming laboured from his attention. He moved his mouth to the other breast, giving it just as much attention.

Tyler's hands trailed down my body, his lips following slowly. By the time he reached the top of my panties, I was desperately needy for release. Tyler sat on his heels and pulled my panties off.

He stared down at me with appreciation. "You are beautiful, Lexi."

The genuine-sounding compliment had me at a loss for words. He ducked down, spreading my legs and burying his face into the apex. At the first swipe of his tongue, I cried out, my hand twisting in his hair while my hips bucked upward. *Oh God.* The pure pleasure this man gave me was nothing I'd ever experienced before, and he hadn't even been inside me yet.

"You're so wet." He groaned, widening my opening with two fingers. "I can't wait to bury myself inside you."

"Yes, Tyler." I moaned. "Please hurry."

"Patience, Lexi."

With his hands and tongue, Tyler worked my body into a frenzy. I felt my climax building. I was right on the edge, ready to fall over with an orgasm. He sucked on my clit. The orgasm crashed over me, and I screamed his name. Tyler lapped up the juices.

Sliding off the bed, he stripped himself of his boxer briefs. I stared wide-eyed at his impressively large cock. I licked my lips, watching as he rolled on a condom he'd grabbed from the bedside table. With complete male confidence, he crawled over me.

"Come on, Tyler." I prodded, wrapping my arms around his neck. "Finish what you started."

"Oh honey, I've only just begun." He promised.

He pulled my hands down, linked our fingers, kissed me and slid inside. Slowly. Inch by delicious inch until he was fully sheathed inside.

"Damn, you feel good." Tyler rested his forehead on mine. "I'm not hurting you, am I?"

I shook my head. "I want more."

"More?"

I hooked a leg over his ass, pushing him forward while I lifted my hips to meet him. Pelvis to pelvis, Tyler's full girth was buried as deep as possible. My head fell back on the pillow, and a satisfied moan escaped.

"You feel so good, Tyler."

"I'll make you feel even better, honey."

Prologue Two

TYLER

I woke with the warm and beautiful Lexi in my arms. She stirred, emitted a soft sigh, and shimmied into me. I tightened my hold on her, keeping her pressed against me and kissed her shoulder.

"Morning, honey."

"Morning." She looked over her shoulder at me. "Do you even remember my name?"

"Of course I do, Lexi." I rolled her under me and kissed her deeply. "I'll never forget it, or you."

"Bold words."

There was doubt in her tone, and nothing I could say would change that. Something happened last night. Meeting Lexi was life-changing, a shock to my system. No woman has ever shaken my soul like she has. Lexi is unique, and I want to see her again and have her in my bed again. It's possible that she could be the one for me. *I'll have to test my theory.*

"Do you have plans today?" I kissed her neck.

"I do." She arched into me.

"With me, I hope." I kissed down her body.

"With a friend."

Her breasts were the perfect size for my hands. She moaned as I messaged them. With my hands staying on her breasts, my kisses continued lower until I reached the haven between her legs.

Lexi gasped. "Oh God, Tyler."

Her hips bucked upward. Bolstered by her obvious pleasure, I continued to taste her sweet nectar. I nearly had Lexi boneless in my bed when there was a ringing in the room.

"That's my phone." Lexi said. "I need to answer it."

Reluctantly, I sat up. Lexi swung her legs over the bed and strode across the room to where she'd dropped her pants. The ringing had stopped ringing by the time she pulled her phone out of the back pocket.

"I should return this call." Lexi stated.

"Go ahead." I repositioned myself in bed, leaning against the headrest.

"Hey, you called?" Lexi said into the phone while collecting her clothes. "I haven't forgotten. I'll be there. If you let me go now, I can start to get ready."

Lexi was on the phone a bit longer before hanging up.

"Was that the friend you have plans with?" I asked.

"Yeah." Lexi got dressed as she spoke. "She knew I got stood up last night and was checking in to make sure I was still good for today."

"Does she know about me? Or at least, does she know you were with me last night?"

"No, she thinks I went home. We talked moments before a very sexy detective offered to keep me company."

Lexi, fully dressed, crawled onto the bed with a mischievous grin. Resting her hands on my chest, she initiated a kiss. Despite the urge to haul her onto my lap, I settled for cupping her face and kissing her back.

Lexi pulled away. "I really should get going."

"I want to see you again."

She hesitated, then smiled. "I think that can be arranged."

"Give me your phone. I'll insert my number."

Again, she hesitated but passed me her phone nonetheless. I added my cell phone number and then texted myself so that I'd have her number on my phone. The need coursing through my body was proof enough for me to prove my theory. For me, this wasn't a one-night stand, and I'll make sure she knows it. Lexi kissed me one last time before leaving.

I stood outside Dagger Designs with the small crowd of family and friends who had shown up. My sister, Roxanne, stood at the front door with a massive smile on her face.

"Welcome, everyone." Rox called out to the crowd. "Thank you for coming to the grand opening of my nail salon. It's taken some time to get to this point, and I'm very excited to be here. When I cut this ribbon, we will be open to take appointments, but today is a day to celebrate and show off all my hard work."

There was polite clapping from the crowd, and then Roxanne cut the ribbon that hung loosely across the door, and the clapping intensified with some people whistling. Rox pulled the door open, and the crowd shuffled inside. A few women halted at the reception desk to make an appointment, but the majority of the crown moved further into the salon. There were women seated behind work tables, which I assumed were Rox's staff, with what appeared to be portfolios open on their table.

Rox had set up a table with little bites of food and sparkling water in champagne flutes. I snagged two champagne flutes and went to track down my sister. She was being passed from our dad to our mom as they hugged her. Proud of their daughter.

"Congratulations, sis." I handed her the champagne flute, then drew her in for a one-armed hug. "The place looks great."

"Thanks, Ty." She smiled at me.

"It looks like you'll have plenty of business tomorrow."

"That'll be the real test." She sipped at her drink. "After these initial appointments, things will settle down until word of mouth gets around."

"I'm sure it won't take long, sweetheart." Mom encouraged.

"You had your staff checked out before you hired them, right?" Dad confirmed.

"Dad." Roxanne scolded, though her smile never faded.

"I'm only looking out for you, Sunbeam."

Her attention was snagged by something across the room, and she excused herself from the conversation. I looked around the space again, proud of my sister's bravery in starting her own business. My eyes landed on the back of a blonde head at the receptionist, and my mind went straight to Lexi. I wondered if she was having fun with her friend today.

"Oh, I hope this place flourishes." Mom said. "It's not easy opening a business."

"She'll do fine." Dad wrapped an arm around her and squeezed her lightly. "Roxanne is our daughter, after all."

"Dad's right." I offered. "Rox won't give up just because it's hard."

Mom sighed, agreeing with us. Dad guided her into the crowd so they could chat with the friends that came. Jaylen walked up to me just then.

"Hey, what kept you? You were supposed to pick me up so I could grab my car." I said. "I had to grab a taxi to the station to collect my car."

"Sorry, I had an errand to run and was running late to the opening." Jaylen looked around. "This place looks nice."

I grinned. "Our hard work to help with the inside paid off."

He laughed. "We helped with the demo on day one. Rox had professionals do everything else."

I shrugged. "We still helped."

After the first half-hour, the crowd slowly started to clear out. Those who came to congratulate Roxanne or to book an appointment had accomplished their task. I'd say at least half of the crowd was gone, while the other half enjoyed the conversations. Jaylen and I wondered over to the food table, surprisingly the quietest spot in the salon.

"So?" Jaylen prompted, stuffing a small sandwich in his mouth. "How was your night? Did you get lucky?"

"Yes." Memories of Lexi came flooding into my mind, and I grinned at my partner. "Ditching you was the best decision I could have made."

"So she was more than a pretty face?" He questioned. "I didn't really get a good look at her."

"I'm glad you didn't. We may have fought over who took her home."

"I'd bet all that that blonde hair of hers made her look angelic as you fucked her."

I resisted the sudden urge to punch him for the crude remark. I have no claim on Lexi, so therefore, I have no right to get pissed. Besides, talking about the women we've slept with is a pastime we've always done. Except, those were women we never planned on seeing again. Lexi is different. I want to see her again.

"The woman was more than a good fuck." I told him. "I felt a connection with her."

Jaylen stared at me a moment, then let out a low whistle. "Ok then. Are you going to see her again?"

"I plan to."

"Jaylen, you came." Roxanne interrupted our conversation.

"Opening a business is big." He stated. "I had to come to congratulate you."

She tucked a strand of her hair behind her ear. "Thanks."

"The crowd is thinning." I said. "Do you want us to help clean up?"

"You don't have to."

"It's not a bother." Jaylen added.

"If you insist." Rox looked at her watch. "In fifteen minutes, can you start taking whatever food is left over to the staff room?"

We nodded and waited fifteen minutes. The salon was nearly empty. Mom had settled in at one of the work tables to have her nails done even if work wasn't supposed to start until tomorrow. Dad sat next to her, keeping her company. Jaylen and I began clearing the remaining food. The staff room was down the hall, where Rox's office, the storage room, and the bathroom were also located. We were nearly done when, to my surprise, Lexi walked in.

"Good, there's still food left." She declared.

"Of course there is." Rox proudly said. "I made sure to order lots so you and the rest of the staff have something to eat after the crowd leaves."

"Oh." Lexi froze when she saw me.

"Lexi, this is my brother Tyler and his work partner Jaylen Parry." Rox introduced. "Guys, this is Lexi Dawson, receptionist extraordinaire. We met in college and became fast friends."

"Hi." I extended my hand. "It's nice to meet you."

"Yes." Lexi answered.

"I guess we'll be seeing a lot of each other."

"I guess."

That was that. When Lexi heard that I was Roxanne's brother, her eyes widened, and I saw the moment disappointment filled her pretty blue eyes. If she was planning on returning to my bed, it wasn't going to happen now. Lexi was putting up a barrier against me. It hurt, but it wasn't going to deter me.

She might be able to ignore the connection I know we made last night, but I can't. I will insert myself into her life as a friend, and when I find an opportunity, I'll convince her to take a second chance at us as a couple. *Lexi, in time, you will become my woman.*

One

LEXI

Three Years Later

I ran my fingers in my hair, pushing it away from my face as I worked on entering the revenue and purchase receipts into Roxanne's logbook. All are manually written, and then they are all entered into a computer program to verify that the numbers are as they should be. I'm so grateful she showed Jenna how she runs Dagger Designs behind the scenes, or else I'd be lost. Two months since Rox has been missing, and I'm starting to lose hope that she will ever be found. Whether Rox is found or not, I am a co-owner of the salon — officially signed the paperwork shortly before she went missing — I will not let this business go under. If she's not found, I feel honour bound to keep the salon running in her memory.

"Lexi."

I looked up to see Nico. He strolled into the office and plopped down in a chair. He looked ragged. His suit was wrinkled, his hair unkempt like he'd been running his hands through it for hours, bags under his eyes were far too dark to be normal, and a five o'clock shadow covered his jaw. I swear he didn't have any facial hair when Roxanne was still around.

"Nico." I said softly. "You look like you haven't slept."

"I got a couple of hours." He admitted running a hand over his face. "I keep seeing her face whenever I close my eyes."

"Still, you should really try to sleep longer. You won't be able to function properly at this rate."

"I'll sleep soundly when I have Roxanne back in my arms."

I frowned. "Nico."

"Don't, Lexi." Nico held up a hand. "What can I do to help?"

I handed Nico an inventory sheet. When Roxanne disappeared, Nico had disappeared, desperate to find his fiancée. In time, he's resurfaced. The leads he was following had dwindled, and I started to see the despair creep into his eyes. Nico would spend time at Dagger Designs as a way to keep Roxanne close, so I gave him small tasks to keep him busy. It also benefitted me.

Nico reached for the paper when his phone made a sound. He pulled it out and sat a little straighter. He immediately dialled someone.

"Where?" He demanded, pausing for an answer. "I'm on my way."

"Nico?" I questioned as he stood.

"There's been a sighting. I'm going to check it out."

He was gone before I could warn him. This was Roxanne's fifth sighting in two months, each one a false lead. Every time Nico's hopes were raised, they were squashed by disappointment. *Please, no more false leads.* I mentally prayed. I don't know if his heart will survive another disappointment. I don't know if I can take any more false hope. I haven't had time to grieve the void Roxanne made when she was kidnapped.

I leaned back in the chair, staring at the ceiling. "Where are you, Rox?"

I looked at the door at the sound of footsteps. Barbara came into view, and I welcomed her into the office. I forced a smile, needing to be strong for those around me. If we all broke down, then none of us would be able to move forward.

"Barb! This is unexpected."

"I just saw Nico rush out of here." She stated, hopefully. "Has Rox been found?"

"Not yet." I shook my head. "He says there's a sighting, but nothing has been confirmed."

"Oh." Her shoulders fell. "Do you have a minute?"

"Of course." I came around the desk to hug her. "Do you need more help with the wedding?"

"Actually." Barb took my hands and looked at the floor nervously. "It's just, um, with Roxanne, um."

"Missing?" I supplied when she began to trail off.

"Yeah." Tears filled Barbara's eyes. "Missing."

I squeezed her hands, encouraging her to continue. Barb and Rox have been best friends since middle school. This void of

Rox's kidnapping has hit her hard, especially with her wedding coming up fast, and Roxanne was part of the bridal party. Barbara and I had become friends thanks to Roxanne, so I offered to help with the wedding.

"I really want Rox at my wedding." Barb choked out. "If she's not, could you take her place?"

"Barb." I said softly, knowing how hard it was to ask.

She looked up at me, pleading with those caramel eyes of hers. Seeing the gap in the bridal party may crush her more than knowing Roxanne won't be there. How could I say no?

"Sure." I agreed, finding that my voice was getting stuck in my throat. "I'll do that for you."

"Thanks."

We fell silent. I hope Tyler or Nico can find Roxanne before Barbara has to walk down the aisle. Barbara mumbled that she had to leave and gave me another hug. I watched her go, wishing there was more that I could do.

"Lexi, I'm heading home."

I waved at Rita. "See you tomorrow."

She nodded and continued out the back door. She was Roxanne's last hire before disappearing, and it was an excellent choice. Rita took on all of Rox's clients and even made a few regulars of her own. She and Dahlia, who only works weekends since going back to school for her twelfth and final year, have been working together to maintain the salon's social media presence. I collected my purse and did one final check of the salon to ensure it was clean and locked up tight before heading out.

I didn't go home. While Tyler worked late trying to find his sister and balancing his regular cases, he asked me to check in on his dog. I pulled into the driveway of Tyler's house, the end unit of a fourplex, and used the key he'd given me to enter. Something about this place feels like home, like I should be doing this on a regular basis, not just to dogsit.

"Lucky!" I called out when I opened the door. "Come here, boy."

The scraping sound of nails on hardwood could be heard racing across the floor. The beagle came to a skidding stop in front of me. His tail wagging happily as I bent to scratch his head.

"Want to go for a walk?"

He barked, sitting down obediently so I could hook a leash to his collar. Tyler trained Lucky well. Once hooked up and I had a few poop bags in my pocket, I led him outside. The weather was just warm enough that a coat wasn't needed. It won't be long before fall is upon us. I smiled to myself, thinking of all the fall shoes I would get to wear soon.

I locked up and then looked down at Lucky. "Okay, boy, let's go."

Lucky trotted a little ahead of me as we walked around the neighbourhood. Tyler had picked Lucky up at a shelter over three years ago. The dog had been abused by its previous owner, so it took time for Lucky to trust him. It surprised us both when Lucky took an immediate shine to me.

"Doggy!" a little girl shrieked with delight.

Lucky froze as she ran toward him with her arms outstretched. He tucked his tail between his legs, and he visibly shook as he stared at the approaching form. I scooped Lucky up off the ground before she got too close. Behind the little girl, her father chased after her.

"No, no, no, no." He chided until he caught up and gently grabbed her arm to hold her back. "You do not chase after animals like that."

"But I wanted to pet him." She pouted.

"What if he's not a friendly dog?"

The little girl looked up at me. "She's holding him."

I smiled softly at her. "It's my dog, he trusts me."

"I'm sorry about her." The father apologized, scooping his daughter into his arms and taking a step back. "Is your dog okay?"

"He will be." I scratched his back. "I think, though, our walk is over."

I returned to the house with Lucky still in my arms. Tyler's car was behind mine when we returned. I put Lucky down in the entry, and he made a beeline for the kitchen. I followed to put the poop bag in the garbage and to wash my hands. Lucky was already chowing down on his food.

"Hey, bud. Did you enjoy your walk?" Tyler questioned the beagle as he bent to pet his head. "Or was it the company?"

Tyler looked up at me, and I felt my cheeks heat. I never got over Tyler after our one night together three years ago. Roxanne learnt about my feelings for her brother not too long before her disappearance and urged me to pursue Tyler. I haven't been able to do it. I want to, but it doesn't feel like the right time. Tyler hasn't made a move, either. *Maybe it's one-sided.*

"Lexi?"

"There was one incident." I shook my head of thoughts of us and explained what happened.

"I see." Tyler stood. "Thank you."

"Oh. Um. It was nothing."

He tilted his head to the side, and his dirty blond hair fell over his green eyes. "Why are you so nervous?"

"I'm not." I squeaked.

"You are. In fact, you've been acting differently around me since that night outside the salon a couple of months ago." He frowned, standing so we were on even ground. "What did my sister say about me that night?"

"Nothing." I put up my hands and took a step back.

"Hmm?" He mused, taking a step forward. "I don't believe that."

"That's not my problem." I countered defensively. "I should get going."

I took another step back. Lucky barked, drawing my attention down and behind me. I didn't hear him move from his food bowl. With my retreat from Tyler and Lucky's sneaky arrival behind me, I tried to correct my backstep, but it was too late, and I tripped over Lucky.

"Lexi."

Tyler reached for me. His arm wrapped my waist, twisting us around so he landed on the hardwood floor instead of me. It all seemed to happen in slow motion. Tyler groaned upon impact while I landed on his chest.

"I'm sorry. Are you okay?"

"I'm fine." He said.

"I'll get off of you." I started to push myself off of him.

"Don't move." He tightened his grip around me.

"Tyler?"

"I've been wanting you in my arms again since that night after the bar three years ago."

I felt my face heat with his confession and buried my reaction in his chest. *Did I hear that right?* Roxanne's voice rang in my mind: If Tyler's the one you can't forget, then go after him. Doing something for myself, something that'll make me happy, seems wrong while my best friend is missing.

"I thought we had a connection." Tyler lifted my face to stare into my eyes. "Was I wrong?"

My throat tightened. He didn't try to pursue me after that one night, so I thought the connection was one-sided. When I didn't answer, he slowly let me go. Hurt and disappointment filled his green eyes. He was misunderstanding my silence. Tyler pushed himself into a sitting position.

Panicked that I might be messing up my second chance with Tyler, I repositioned myself on his lap. Facing him, with my legs wrapped around his waist, I captured his face in my hands and kissed him. He was hesitant, as if uncertain as to why I was kissing him. Tyler didn't kiss me back, but he wasn't pushing me away either. *I need to explain.*

"No, Tyler, you're not wrong." I told him, holding his gaze so he could see the truth of my words. "I was afraid."

His brows drew together. "Afraid of what?"

"Of what would happen if we didn't work out."

"I don't understand."

"Your sister is my best friend." I explained. My eyes dropped to his chest, where my fingers had lowered to play with the top button of his dress shirt nervously. "I didn't want her to choose between us if we broke up. Seeing you all the time after we broke up because of our connection to Rox would be awkward and painful. I didn't want to go through that."

"Lexi." Tyler said softly, lifting my chin. "What if we never broke up?"

"I don't know." I shrugged. "I didn't really consider it. I'm not very good with relationships."

"You better start considering it." He said. "I still want you, Lexi. I never stopped wanting you."

With that confession, Tyler slanted his lips on mine and kissed me like a starving man desperate to consume his fill. I had no resistance to him. My body lit up as if a switch had turned on. I needed this man to ease every sexual ache I've been holding back since that one night so long ago.

Tyler stood from the floor, my ankles locked behind him as he carried me upstairs to his bedroom. His muscles bunched with every step. The next thing I knew, Tyler was settling my feet to the floor.

"Too many clothes." He mumbled as he pulled back far enough to ease my t-shirt over my head.

Two

TYLER

I woke up instantly, aware of Lexi in my bed and completely satisfied with her curled into me. She smelled of sex and vanilla, making my mouth water and my cock twitch with a need to be inside her again.

"Morning." Lexi's groggy voice held a smile as she wiggled closer.

"Lexi." I groaned.

"What's wrong, Tyler?"

"You know exactly what's wrong."

I have no control when it comes to this woman. *I need her.* Reaching behind me for a condom from the bedside table, I used my teeth to open the package before rolling it on blindly. Lexi giggled at my efforts. Her giggle morphed into a moan as

I drew her leg over mine and slid slowly into her as my hand played with her clit.

Lexi reached back, her nails digging into my ass, a silent plea for me to move. I kissed her neck, moving my hips slowly to not hurt her. Lexi's body reacted to me and my touch like a dream. It didn't take her long to become slick enough for me to move more freely in her.

"Come for me, honey." I ordered, shifting the angle and picking up speed.

"Yes, Tyler." She moaned.

Lexi's hand came down to play with her clit. I moved my hand up to cup her breast, rolling the nipple between my fingers. Lexi cried out and came around me. I repositioned us so she lay beneath me, then sank back into her heat. Gripping her hips, I pounded into her hard and fast until we both came. Breathing heavily, I rolled onto my back.

Lexi turned, resting her head on my chest. "We need a shower."

I ran my hand gently along her spine. "Yes, we do."

"In a minute, though."

"Whenever you're ready, honey."

Lexi frowned, her finger tracing a figure eight on my chest. "Um, last night and this morning was fun."

"But?" I prompted, sensing her pulling away.

"Where does that leave us?"

"I want a relationship with you, Lexi."

She looked up at me. "You do?"

"I do." I placed my hand over hers. "What about you?"

She hesitated. "I want to try."

It was a start. From here on out, I'll do everything in my power to convince her of what I believe to be true. Lexi Dawson is the one for me. Three years ago, she seemed to be looking for something. I'm not sure if she found it or not, but something is still holding her back. The door to her heart has been unlocked for me so I can step in and provide light to her shadows. Lexi is my future. I knew this three years ago, and last night only solidified my resolve. *I won't let you run away this time.*

"How about that shower?" I asked.

Lexi smiled. "Sounds refreshing."

I grinned, pulling her out of bed with me. Taking a shower will never be the same now that I've had one with Lexi Dawson. Lathering her up in soap and kissing every inch of clean skin is how I want to spend every morning.

Clean, dried, and dressed, we made our way to the kitchen. I filled Lucky's bowl with fresh water and the other with fresh food while Lexi pulled out cereal for our breakfast. I put the kettle on and pulled out two mugs and a coffee cone with a filter.

"It's not fancy." I said. "But do you want a cup of coffee?"

Both of our phones interrupted this perfect morning. My phone call was Jaylen letting me know of a murder at a private airstrip. I hung up and looked at Lexi, who was finishing her phone call.

"Can you move your car?" She asked. "I have to get home."

"Is everything okay?"

"I'm not sure. That was Barbara, but she wasn't making any sense."

I turned the kettle off. "I have to head out myself. Let me grab my gear and walk you out."

I collected my gun and badge from the drawer safe in the kitchen, where I'd put them last night before Lexi returned from her walk with Lucky. My keys and wallet were by the door. I'd have liked to take Lucky for a walk, but my beagle will have to settle with the backyard until I get home tonight. Lexi tidied up the kitchen while I collected my things. At her car, I gave her a deep kiss to remember me for the day.

"I hope things aren't serious with Barbara, and whatever it is can be solved easily."

"Me too." She said.

IVY MARIE

Crime scene investigators — better known as CSIs — were busy documenting and collecting evidence when I arrived at the private airstrip. Jaylen was watching them from a short distance, waiting for them to clear out so he could get closer to the body. I stood next to my partner and surveyed the scene. It was clean. The only thing out of place was our murdered victim, taped to a chair and aside from the bullet hole in his forehead, he looked like he was someone's punching bag.

"What happened here?" I asked.

"Besides the obvious?" Jaylen turned, signalling me to follow. "You better come see what the cameras caught."

He led me to an office and sat in a chair. I watched as the surveillance video was rewound. Jaylen hit play. A very familiar face came into view. He seemed to be having a civil conversation until it wasn't. The victim was hauled over the counter by his shirt. Something was shown to him, and then something was pointed out to him. Whatever it was, it was taken. The victim said something and was rewarded with a right hook to the face.

"Well, fuck." I cursed, a rarity for me.

"He should be behind bars." Jaylen accused.

"We tried that, remember?" I scowled at him. "It led to my sister's recklessness and kidnapping."

"He's a wild beast, and your damned deal set him free."

My jaw tightened. *He's not wrong.* When Roxanne went missing, so did Nico, and during that time, injured bodies started surfacing. No one spoke about who beat them to a bloody pulp, but I suspected it was Nico in his search for Roxanne. I also believe the only thing stopping him from killing anyone in his way was his love for Rox. If he were behind bars, he wouldn't be able to save her. My gut tells me Nico is needed to save Roxanne, so I've been doing what I can to keep him out of jail.

I pulled out my phone to call Nico. No answer. Next, I called the station's IT department and had them trace Nico's phone. He was found, or at least his phone was found, at a gym called Rocco's. Before Jaylen and I headed over to talk to him, I wanted another look at the crime scene.

The CSIs were wrapping up, and the coroner was stepping in to handle the body. The victim's face was a puffed-up mess. We might not be able to get any facial recognition. We'll have to rely on dental and fingerprints. Whatever information he was withholding either went with him when he was shot or he was shot after providing the information. We'll never know. *I hope this doesn't lead to another murder.*

I went over to the desk and pulled a clipboard closer. It was faint, but there were imprints from the previous page. I had CSIs bag it for testing. This airstrip's office only has one entrance, and since I didn't see anyone else on the security feed Jaylen had rewound, the murder was either erased or it happened elsewhere. There wasn't much Jaylen or I could do until evidence was analyzed to give us a good stepping stone.

The coroner provided his initial report before having the body taken away for a proper autopsy. There was no need for Jaylen and myself to stick around, so we went to Rocco's. Rocco's is a three-story brick building on the edge of Frostham's industrial area.

"Let's split up." Jaylen said after flashing our badge at Rocco's receptionist.

"Sure. Remember, we're here to talk to Nico, not start a fight."

He grunted and stalked off in the direction of the pool. On the outside, Rocco's is unassuming, but inside is clean and modern. Roxanne had brought me here a few times as her guest, and we always went rock climbing. *Would Nico be rock climbing?* I shook my head, dismissing that idea. He seems more of a weights and punching bag kind of man.

I went to the third floor, where most of the exercise equipment was located. The second floor has a running track, a boxing ring, wrestling mats and various punching bags. I glanced around the space as I passed by and almost missed Nico. He had bent down to pick up a water bottle and was coming to stand when I was about to continue to the top floor.

"There you are." I crossed my arms, stopping next to the punching bag he was using. "We have to talk."

"You could have called me, Baxter." He responded.

"I did."

He wiped his face with a towel. "I would have called you back."

"It's about the private airstrip."

Nico's jaw tightened as he glared at me. Clearly, he wasn't going to tell me anything that easily. I eyed him, trying to determine if he knew about the murder or not.

"Care to tell me why you were at the airstrip?" I asked.

"Following a lead."

"A lead that ended in a murder." Jaylen growled, joining us.

"Murder?" Nico echoed in surprise. "I haven't murdered anyone."

"I doubt that."

The two men stood toe-to-toe. I stepped between them, pushing them apart. They've been at each other's throats since Roxanne admitted her love for Nico, and then she wore an engagement ring the next day. Jaylen's hatred for Nico, as I learnt after my sister's disappearance, was because he had a relationship with her. A relationship I didn't know about. I'm not too keen about my sister having a relationship with Nico Frangione, but at least his relationship was in the open compared to Jaylen. Sort of. I think Dad is the only one in the dark when it comes to his daughter's life, love or social life.

"Let's try this again, Nico." I said. "Why were you at the airstrip?"

Nico ground his teeth. "It'll be easier to show you."

"Show us what?"

"It's on my phone."

We followed him back through the gym to the changing rooms. I stopped Jaylen from following. There's no alternative exit, so I'm not worried about him bolting.

"How long are you going to be like this?" I nagged Jaylen.

"Like what?" He countered.

"Bitter."

"I'm not bitter."

"How would you describe your attitude these past couple of months?"

"Pissed would be the proper word." Jaylen growled, spinning to face me and throwing his hands up. "Roxanne is a smart, beautiful woman. We were together for a year, then this criminal showed up, and she became engaged after a month."

Nico exited the changing room. "I treated Roxanne like the strong, independent woman that she is. Lei è il mio sole."

"See? It's that Italian crap that clouded her mind."

Did Jaylen just insult Roxanne? Right after complimenting her? It irritated me, but I didn't show any reaction. This isn't my fight to fight. Not until I can have a proper conversation with my sister. I want to hear the truth and reasoning from her. Then, and only then, will I defend one of these men.

"Or I just gave her something that you couldn't." Nico countered.

"Okay, that's enough." I snapped. "Until my sister is returned, I don't want to hear the two of you bicker over her anymore. Before she was kidnapped, she chose Nico, a decision I am certain she did not make lightly."

"Thank you." Nico's lips twitched upward.

I glared at him. "I'm withholding final judgment until Roxanne is returned to her family."

Jaylen crossed his arms defiantly. "Fine. I'll agree to a truce until Rox is returned."

"What did you have to show us, Nico?"

He pulled out his phone and then turned it our way. "Yesterday, this was sent to me."

I took the phone and stared at a picture of Roxanne. *She's alive.* Not that I believed she was murdered or anything. My throat went dry. After two months, I was beginning to lose hope, but that wouldn't have stopped me from finding an answer. I just needed to know that she was alive.

"When was this taken?" I forced the question out.

"Two days ago." Nico said.

"What does this have to do with the airstrip?" Jaylen's patience is on edge.

Nico reached over and swiped to show us more pictures: Roxanne smiling at someone, Roxanne being kissed by someone, and then a clear shot of Franco Frangione with his arm around Roxanne. The final few pictures were of them entering a small plane. One of those pictures showed the tail number.

"That was why I was at the airstrip." Nico took his phone back. "I was there to find the flight plan."

"We need these pictures and whatever information you took from the airstrip." I told him.

He handed over a piece of paper. "This is the flight plan."

Jaylen snatched the paper from his suit pocket. "There's no destination listed."

"Franco would have made sure of that."

Nico was holding something back. I wanted to press him but didn't think he'd tell me anything with Jaylen right here. I'll need to corner him later. If he knew anything more about my sister's location, he wouldn't be able to hide it from me. That, I am sure of. Somehow, since Roxanne's car accident, which led to a kidnapping, Nico and I gained a tentative respect for each other.

Three

LEXI

AFTER BARBARA'S PHONE CALL, I rushed home. I wanted to get changed before she showed up. I tossed my purse over the back of the couch and continued to the bedroom. There was a knock at the front door. With a groan, I turned around to answer it.

"Barbara, come on in." I swept an arm into my apartment. "You got here faster than I expected."

"I may have run a red light or two on my way over." She admitted.

I studied her flushed face and red eyes. Concerned, I took her over to the couch. Whatever had her a babbling mess over the phone didn't have anything to do with her wedding. It was much more severe. *What could this be about?*

"Talk to me, Barb."

"It's Roxanne."

My throat tightened. "What about her?"

"She's alive." Barb held my hands tightly.

"What do you mean?" I didn't understand.

"She's alive, Lexi."

"Of course, she's alive." I said, there was no doubt of that fact in my voice.

"Did Tyler or Nico tell you something?" She leaned in expectantly.

"No, they didn't. It's just a gut feeling. I always believed Rox was alive. She only needed to be found."

"Oh. Well, she's been found."

"Did you tell Tyler?"

"No." Barb shook her head. "A nurse friend of mine saw her."

I remained silent. This could be another false sighting. Until Tyler or Nico tell me otherwise, I find it hard to believe a third-party source. Though, this is Barbara. I doubt she would accept just anyone's word who claims they saw Roxanne. *Gather the information, then pass it along.*

"Okay." I said softly as if talking to a skittish bunny. "What did this friend of yours say?"

Barbara started to tear up. "It's horrible, Lexi."

I pulled her into a hug, rubbing her back. "Start from the beginning. Tell me everything."

"My friend." She sniffled, trying to regain her composure. "She had been hired for a private nursing job."

"That can be done?" I interrupted.

"If the client has enough money or influence within the hospital." Barbara explained. "It's rare, but doctors and nurses can be bought out for their services."

I nodded. "How long was this private nursing job?"

"Two months. It ended two days ago." She wiped at her cheeks as fresh tears started again. "Roxanne was her patient."

"Your friend's patient? Are you sure it was Roxanne?"

Barbara nodded. "She was in a coma."

A coma. It was a lot to take in. It was even harder to accept. I sat there with Barbara, not saying a word as I comforted her by simply holding her hand. When she seemed more composed, I tried to get more information from her about where Roxanne was being held and about who was keeping her from her family. Barbara, or at least her nurse friend, didn't know much. But the name Frangione did come up a few times in hushed conversations between the doctor and a man.

"What should we do?" Barbara asked me as if I had all the answers.

"Nothing." I said.

"But, Roxanne."

"You don't know where Rox has been these past couple of months — as in, the exact location." I said far more calmly than I felt. "If your friend was let go two days ago, then I'm going to assume that Rox has been moved."

"But I can find out where my friend worked. Then we can go and maybe find something that'll lead us in the right direction." She hedged.

"Barbara, we're not detectives."

"Her brother is, though." Barbara stated, her shoulders straightening. "He could come with us to find her."

"Yes, he is a detective, and I will tell him everything you told me." I told her. "You and I are not going to do anything more than that, especially you. You have a wedding to get ready for, and it's only a few short months away."

"Three, to be exact." She corrected, then started tearing up again. "I hate this. I want to help."

"I know." I soothed, knowing exactly how she felt. "Do you tell Liz everything you told me?"

"You mean my prosecutor sister?" Barbara let out a harsh laugh. "I wasn't sure if she'd be more sister or prosecutor."

"It involves Roxanne. I'm sure she'll be more sisterly."

"Maybe." She mumbled.

We sat in silence, holding each other's hands for emotional support. I wanted to be there for Barb. She had known Roxanne long before I did. Except I can't. Being a strong, supportive friend is fine, but it's weighing me down. *When will I get to cry?*

"Barb." I pulled my hands away. "I need to get ready for work."

"Yes, right, I'm sorry." Barbara collected herself and stood.

I walked her to the door, giving her one last hug before closing the door behind her. Now I can finally change into fresh clothes. I probably beat a world record for changing clothes, excluding quick-change artists where it's their specialty. I grabbed a granola bar and my purse, then locked my apartment.

> **Rita:** Are you coming in today?

> **Me:** Leaving my place now.

> **Rita:** I want to run something by you when you come in.

Half an hour later, I parked my car in the staff parking lot behind Dagger Designs. I put my purse in the office and then walked onto the salon floor. It was only a Thursday morning, and every nail technician had a client, leaving the receptionist's desk unattended. Everyone had stepped up since Rox's disappearance. They all took turns answering the phone and greeting the clients as they walked in.

I slid onto the bar stool behind the receptionist's desk and let out a little sigh. I miss this spot. Being the receptionist brought me inner peace, but since I had to do paperwork in the office, I've been behind this desk less and less. Dahlia held the position in the summer after she completed Clavus Schola, the nail school Rox sponsored her into. Now, she only works weekends.

Before I knew it, it was lunchtime. I called Tyler and told him about everything Barbara told me. I hope he can do something with it.

"Lexi, is now a good time to talk?" Rita slipped into the breakroom.

I stopped my search of the fridge for something to eat and gave her my full attention. "What is it, Rita?"

"Well, I was wondering if we could do something fun on Dagger Designs' social media."

"Like what?"

"A competition." She took a seat at the small table, and I joined her. "It could be themed, and then all of the nail techs would make a set of nails on the practice hands to be posted. Then, all of our followers could vote for their favourite, and that tech would win something."

"What would they win?"

"I'm not sure." Rita admitted. "Or we could make it city-wide. Have the best nail tech from various nail salons in Frostham compete in a bracket-style competition, and again, the voting would be done through social media. This might even boost other salons."

"They are both interesting ideas." I tapped my nails along the table's surface. "But they also sound like a lot of work."

"I have a friend in the event industry. She'd know how to plan either one of these ideas."

"If you can work with her to get me a project outline of how either event would work and how much, if any, it would cost to do." I said. "I'll review the proposals, and we can maybe set something up for next year."

Rita smiled. "Okay. Thank you, Lexi."

I returned to the fridge, opened the freezer top and pulled out a pizza pocket. It's not ideal, but it's quick and should give me enough energy to last until supper time.

Four

TYLER

JAYLEN AND I RETURNED to the station after talking with Nico. I couldn't let myself be distracted by the idea of Roxanne being in the arms of Franco. It's far more disturbing than my sister being with Nico. I spread out pictures of the crime scene across my desk and went over the report of collected evidence. Somewhere here, there will be a clue that we can follow up on.

"That tail number is registered to Enzo Frangione." Jaylen announced. "I knew that bastard was hiding something."

"So, Nico probably knows where the plane went." I said, making a mental note to bring it up when I visited Nico later.

"I'm going to talk to him again."

"Focus on the murder."

Jaylen glared at me. "I don't get you."

I looked up at my partner." Don't get what?"

"How can you be so calm after seeing those pictures? Don't you want to be out there searching? This is your sister we're talking about."

"Of course I do." I slammed my fist onto my desk, drawing unwanted attention. I lowered my voice. "We have no guarantee about when those pictures were taken."

Jaylen paused. "You think Nico lied about when he received those pictures?"

"No, not when it comes to Roxanne. The guy that took them could be lying about when he saw Rox with Franco."

"Then let's go talk to this private investigator."

"You don't know who he is, and Nico won't tell you." I frowned, looking at the pictures.

"I'll make him talk." Jaylen said confidently, cracking his knuckles.

I brought a picture up to my face and then handed it to my partner. "Does that look like ash to you?"

Jaylen took the picture. "Maybe. Was it collected?"

"I think so." I reviewed the evidence report. "Yes, here it is."

"Then it'll be analyzed."

That pile of ash bothered me. It reminded me of the cigar ash found in Rox's car the night she went missing. It was a small pile. We'd almost missed it, thinking it was just dirt or sand, but it was a clue that unfortunately led nowhere credible. Except the ash came from a rare and expensive imported cigar brand. The company that sells them refused to give us a customer list, and since they aren't local to Frostham, we couldn't execute a warrant to get the list.

Something about this murder feels off. The question that I want to have answered is, why kill the airstrip employee? The answer to that will direct us to the who aspect of this case. The why is challenging without knowing who the victim is. There was no wallet on the victim, no name tag on his shirt, and no employment record in the office. Jaylen settled back in his chair. We need to work with what we have, which isn't much. Until the coroner gets back to us with an identification for our victim, there's not much we can do.

"Baxter." I answered my ringing phone without looking at the caller ID.

"Tyler."

I sat up a little straighter. "Lexi. Did you talk to Barbara? How is she?"

"She's distressed." Lexi admitted. "She told me that Roxanne has been in a coma in a private facility for the past two months."

"How did she come by that information?"

"A friend of hers was hired to be a private nurse. She was let go two days ago."

That timeline nearly matches the pictures Nico received from his PI. "I'll look into it, Lexi. Things might get a little hectic."

"I'll take care of Lucky."

"Thanks, Lexi." I smiled. "I'll keep you as updated as possible."

"One more thing. Barb's friend heard Frangione's name. No first name."

"Interesting."

51

I hung up and pushed back my chair. *I wonder if Nico knows about this.* It's time to talk to Nico again. Alone.

"Where are you going?" Jaylen asked.

"Out. There's something I need to check up on."

"How's Lexi been holding up?"

I grimaced. "Surprisingly well put together. She's kept herself busy with the salon."

Lexi cried the day I told her the news about Roxanne, then carried on as if my sister was away on vacation. Actually, now that I think about it, Lexi didn't really let herself cry. Her eyes watered, and she was visibly distraught, but no tears fell. I shook my head, mostly clearing it of thoughts of Lexi, and refocused on the conversation I needed to have with Nico.

"Where are you right now?" I called Nico while in the privacy of my car. "We need to talk. Off the books."

"Must be important."

"Location, Nico."

"I'll meet you at Croquette. Go in through the back."

I followed his instructions. It was too early for the restaurant to be open, so we wouldn't have to worry about being overheard or seen. Fresh produce was being brought in, supervised by Nico's cousin, who owned the restaurant. He recognized me and let me go through the kitchen, telling me that Nico was waiting for me. I found Nico at a table drinking a glass of water.

"So, what did you need to talk to me about?" He asked.

"Roxanne."

He sat up a little straighter. "What about her?"

"I've been given some information that I want to go over with you."

"Okay." Nico gripped his glass tighter. "What did you learn?"

"She's been in a coma, monitored by a private nurse who was let go two days ago. The Frangione name was heard while the nurse was working." I told him, watching closely for his reaction. "Then, of course, there are the pictures of Roxanne boarding a Frangione plane that you showed me. The timelines coincide with each other."

"That is quite a lot of information."

Nico ran a hand through his hair. Upon closer inspection, I could see how ragged he looked. There were bags under his eyes and a growing beard on his face. He didn't look as suave as he normally did. Not having Roxanne around is really impacting the lives of everyone who knows her.

"Here's my theory." I leaned forward, clasping my hands together and placing them on the table. "Franco orchestrated Rox's car accident so he could take her away. For two months, he kept her in a private facility with a well-paid doctor and nurse to keep an eye on her. Whatever they were doing was complete, so the doctor and nurse were let go, and Rox was flown somewhere private."

"That's a well-thought-out theory." Nico acknowledged.

"How much of it is accurate?"

"Franco took Roxanne to a private island." He held up a hand. "Before you say anything, I didn't go after them because there is no way I wouldn't have been noticed. That damned picture of Roxanne smiling and being kissed by Franco is bothering me."

"What do you think Franco did to her during those two months?" I questioned, frowning because I didn't want to think of the possibilities.

"I don't know exactly what Franco would do to her." Nico admitted. "The worst-case scenario is all my mind can conjure, and it's only made scarier because I know what Franco is capable of."

I gulped. "I'm afraid to ask, but what is your worst-case scenario?"

"It's better you don't know."

"Nico."

"Trust me."

I glared at him. If he didn't want me to be curious, he shouldn't have said anything. Now, my mind is going to conjure every possible scenario and steadily get worse until I have an answer.

"Fine." I ground out. "Then, do you know when the Frangione plane is to return?"

Nico seemed to relax with the change of topic. "The plane is scheduled to return in a week."

"In the meantime, we can track down the doctor and find out exactly what happened to my sister."

"We?" He raised a brow.

"You have the connections to find this doctor. I have the badge to make him talk."

Nico chuckled.

"Or keep you out of jail." I added.

"Thanks, Baxter."

Five

LEXI

I BARELY SAW TYLER all week. He'd send me a text, or two during the day, but that's about all the communication I'd get from him. Lucky talked to me more when I went over to walk the dog. *Is this what a relationship with Tyler is like?* Maybe all we really have is a sexual connection.

The only way to know is to ask. How do I bring it up in conversation? What if I'm expecting too much, and by talking about my insecurities, I'll ruin whatever we have? Too many questions that lead to negative answers keep rolling around in my head. I used to go to Roxanne for all my issues with the male species, and she'd set me straight.

I sat on Tyler's couch, feet tucked under me and scrolled through my phone. I opened the dating app I used to use often until last week when Tyler said he wanted a relationship with me. It's not that I'm looking for a date. I only want to see who else is out there. Lucky jumped onto the couch, settled himself in the crook of my knees and rested his head on my thigh.

"What do you think of this guy?" I showed Lucky a picture, and he growled in response. "Yeah, you're right. There are too many muscles. He's probably a gym rat."

I continued scrolling through the app. *I should delete this from my phone.* None of the men appealed to me. Being back in Tyler's bed has ruined the appeal of other men. I laid my head against the back of the couch and idly scratched Lucky's head. Who am I kidding? Tyler has been the standard for three years. Still, I brought the phone up and stared at a good-looking guy with glasses and a dimple on his cheek. The dimple was cute.

"Who is this?" Tyler plucked the phone from my hand.

"Tyler!"

I jolted, twisting to see him. I didn't even hear him approach, let alone come into the house. Lucky growled softly at my sudden movement, then hopped off the couch. The beagle settled himself in his bed on the ground. I shifted up onto my knees, reaching over the back of the couch for my phone. Tyler kept the device out of my reach, a frown forming as he perused my profile on the dating app.

"Give me back my phone." I demanded.

"Why do you need a dating app anyway?"

"So I can date, duh." I responded with a roll of my eyes.

Something unreadable flashed in his eyes. "Delete the app, Lexi."

I was considering it, but because he was ordering me to do it, I bristled. Glaring defiantly, I answered him.

"Why should I?"

"Because you have me." Tyler grabbed the back of my neck and kissed me possessively. "Delete the app, Lexi."

My head spun with that kiss. "Ask me again."

Tyler's lips quirked up as he kissed me again. He coaxed my lips apart and swept his tongue inside. Angling his head, his kiss went deeper. I gripped the back of the couch, trying to stop myself from melting into the piece of furniture. When he finally let me up for air, I took in deep, shuttering breaths, and his green eyes darkened to a gorgeous forest green.

"Now, about that dating app."

"What dating app?" I smiled at him.

"Good girl." He whispered, giving my lips a quick peck.

I took the phone back. Shutting down the app, I tucked the device into the back pocket of my jeans. Tyler glared at me.

"What?" I asked.

"The app."

"I'll delete it later. I have to go in and delete my profile first."

He crossed his arms over his chest. "I can wait."

I scowled at him. "Is this what being in a relationship with you is really like? I barely hear from you all week. I don't see you at all, and when I do, you're ordering me around."

"Lexi." His features softened. "I'm sorry."

"Because if it is, then I don't want any part of it." I continued. "I want to be with someone who can make time for me."

"I was looking into the private facility you told me about."

"Oh." I felt embarrassed by my outburst.

"I'm sorry I made you feel unwanted. Believe me, that's the last thing I ever want to do." Tyler caressed my cheek. "Will you forgive me if I tell you everything I learned?"

"Maybe."

His smile was fleeting as he turned on his cop face, as Roxanne had deemed it. His eyes went hard, and his expression neutral. I didn't see his cop face often, and I'm glad I didn't. It's actually scary how he shifts into a completely different personality.

"You might want to sit down." He gently pushed at my shoulders.

"Is it that bad?" I sat down, my gaze following him as he came around to sit next to me. "Was it a false lead?"

"No, it wasn't."

"Tell me everything, Tyler, don't hold anything back."

He searched my face before giving a slight nod. "Rox was injured in that accident, which gave Franco an opening to have one of his men kidnap her from the scene. Franco hired a doctor, paying him a lot of money, to keep her in a coma."

"Oh God." My hands flew to my mouth, covering a sob that bubbled up in my throat.

"Nico received pictures from a PI that showed Rox boarding a plane with Franco."

"When?"

"Last week."

A memory of Nico leaving the Dagger Designs office in a rush last week suddenly came forward. "I remember. Nico was at the salon when he received that message. At least, I think that's why he left so suddenly. All he said was that there was a sighting, and he was checking it out."

Tyler's brow went up, but he didn't comment. "Apparently, Nico followed that lead to a private airstrip and learned about the flight. The man he confronted about the plane and the flight plan turned up dead soon after."

"He didn't do it." I defended instantly.

Tyler scowled at my quick response. "I know, but the evidence is against him right now."

I took hold of his hands. "Then he's being set up."

"I know." He said with a sigh, lacing his fingers in mine. "He may be a criminal, but he's not a killer."

My lips thinned. There's something more in the underlining of his words. As much as I wanted to explore what it is, I chose not to broach the subject. For now, I should focus on Roxanne.

"After you called me with Barbara's story." Tyler continued. "I reached out to Nico. We've been working on tracking down the doctor and the private facility."

"That's how you confirmed Rox was in a coma?"

"This is where the story takes a turn." He took a deep breath, steadying himself before breaking the news. His cop face was replaced with that of a concerned brother. "The induced coma was done to force memory loss."

My brows knitted. "Memory loss?"

"When Roxanne awoke from her coma, she couldn't remember a small time frame of her life. The doctor can't say exactly how much is missing, but he said that her husband would be able to help her remember."

"Husband? Rox isn't married."

"Franco Frangione is taking full advantage."

It took a moment before I understood what he meant, and I gasped. The impact of Rox believing she's married to Franco will be catastrophic for Nico. Then, what about her family? What lies will Franco tell her about them? Will it even be possible to get Roxanne back? There are too many questions bouncing around in my head. I felt myself starting to spiral. My breathing picked up, panicking that Rox may never be returned to us. I need her.

I vaguely registered Tyler calling my name. I didn't notice when he cupped my face, forcing me to look at him. I tried to focus on his green eyes. I tried to calm myself. Couldn't. Then, Tyler kissed me. His lips were on mine, slowly bringing me back. I felt the inner storm calm with his embrace and leaned into him.

"Are you okay?" He asked, resting his forehead against mine.

"Thank you." I whispered.

"I'm sorry. I shouldn't have burdened you with everything at once."

"I needed to know. I asked you to tell me."

"Nico and I will do everything we can to bring Roxanne home." Tyler vowed. "It may take some time, but Franco will not win."

The dams broke. I couldn't hold back the tears any longer. Tyler pulled me onto his lap. He held me and rocked me gently, soothing me as I cried into his chest. Only with Tyler will I ever show this weakness. Only with Tyler do I feel strong enough to be this weak.

Six

TYLER

LEXI CRIED HERSELF TO exhaustion. Lifting her in my arms, I carried her to my bed. This is the first time I've seen her cry. Truly cry, not just tear up. It broke my heart to see those tears. Even though I knew it had to do with Roxanne's situation, I still put those tears in her eyes. I also felt humbled that she cried in my presence. She doesn't seem like the kind of person who shows any weakness to anyone. I silently vowed never to have Lexi cry again unless they were tears of happiness.

I laid Lexi down, brushing my thumb along her cheek to wipe at the dried-up tear tracks. Lexi tilted her face into my touch. I hate seeing her in this state. Almost broken, yet refusing to break. From the moment she first smiled at me that day all those years ago, I knew I'd do anything to keep that smile. *Tears don't suit her.*

"Tyler." Lexi murmured when I began to pull away.

"I'm right here, honey." I assured her.

"Need you."

Those two words were said so quietly that I almost didn't hear them. It steeled my resolve to make Lexi mine forever. Lexi Dawson will be Lexi Baxter. In order to convince her that it won't ruin her friendship with my sister, I need to get Roxanne back so she can assure Lexi that marrying me won't change what they have.

I pulled the sheet back and laid down next to Lexi. She instantly wrapped her hands into my shirt and snuggled close. I held her in my arms. Sleep came to me slowly as my mind worked on sorting through my options for what to do next.

In the morning, Lexi acted as though she never had a weak moment yesterday. She was back to her strong, brave self. We were able to have breakfast together and took Lucky for a walk before going our separate ways.

I didn't get a chance to settle in at my desk. Captain Baxter flung his office door open and summoned me. I glanced at my partner, who only shrugged. My greeting to my dad cut off as I took in who else was in the room. Chief of Police Patrick Mann and Mayor Arnie Jones. *This can't be good.* The atmosphere in the room was heavy, and neither one of them held a hint of warmth. Whatever this is, it is serious.

"Close the door, Detective Baxter." Patrick ordered.

I obeyed. "Am I in trouble?"

"We just want to ask you some questions." Patrick stood from the chair he was occupying and moved to stand behind my Captain. "Let's start with the murder at the airstrip."

"Not much to say. The cause of death was a gunshot execution style. My partner and I are still trying to find someone who'd have a reason to kill him." I explained.

"What about Nico Frangione?" Captain Baxter asked while turning his computer my way. "The security cameras caught him roughing up the murder victim."

"Detective Parry and I did question Nico Frangione." I said, maintaining a calm composure. "There is no evidence to indicate that he was the murderer."

"Frangione could have been brought in for assault." Patrick stated. "I knew that making a deal with him was a bad idea."

"Nico was right." I defended. "Something did happen to my sister. Therefore, all charges against him were dropped as agreed upon."

"Yes, your sister. Let's talk about that for a minute."

I clenched my hands at my sides. *Is this the real reason I was called in here?* I glanced at my dad. His shoulders stiffened, and his jaw tightened. He didn't like the direction this was going either. I returned my gaze to Patrick. His grey eyes glimmered, and there was a ghost of a smirk on his lips. He was savouring this moment. I frowned. Something about this didn't feel right.

"Your sister has been missing for two months." Patrick stated. "You've used police resources to try and find her, and you've been harassing the missing person department about not being able to find her."

"Patrick." Mayor Jones spoke for the first time. "What is the point you are trying to make?"

"After all this time, there have been no leads to find her. Drop the search and focus on the job you're paid to do."

"Not happening." I snarled, pulling out my phone. "I have photographic evidence that she's alive. I also spoke to a doctor who admits that he helped to keep her in a coma."

Dad and Mayor Jones sucked in breaths. The news is shocking. I nearly socked the doctor after hearing his tale. Patrick was the only one who remained impassive. No, that's not right. His grey eyes blazed with fury, every muscle taught with anger. If he hadn't been standing behind my dad, he would have noticed and probably questioned the Chief of Police's reaction.

"If this is all true, then you should pass the evidence along to the missing person department." Patrick said. "Let them do their job."

I glared at him. "I'm going to follow up on my lead."

"Then I'm afraid, Detective Baxter, that you are put on immediate leave."

"What?"

"Patrick." Mayor Jones tried to soothe. "Is that really necessary?"

"Yes, it is." Patrick stated firmly. "There will be an internal affairs review of your recent conduct to determine if you should be officially let go."

"This is bullshit." I snarled.

"Gun and badge."

I shot a glance at my dad, at my Captain.

"Where did you get this information about your sister?" Captain Baxter asked.

I hesitated. "There are two sources. One of them is Nico Frangione."

Nothing more could be said. I could see the rigid set of his jaw and the hatred in his eyes. Anything to do with Frangione was tainted. *What will he do when he learns of Rox's engagement to Nico?* It's a secret that everyone except him knows about. Unless he does know and would prefer to ignore it as a factless rumour. I unclipped my badge and gun from my belt and slammed them onto Dad's desk.

"Your hatred is going to cost you." With those final words, I left.

"Ty?" Jaylen questioned as I collected a couple of things from my desk. "Where are you going? What happened in there?"

"I've been put on immediate leave."

"What?" Jaylen bounded to his feet. "Why?"

"Just do your job and catch the criminal." I put a hand on his shoulder and squeezed.

"Tyler."

I lowered my voice. "I'll get Rox back."

His nod was barely perceptible. For the sake of my job, my family, and Lexi, I have to bring Roxanne home.

Seven

LEXI

I FELT DRAINED, PROBABLY from all the crying I did yesterday. I couldn't believe I cried myself to the point of exhaustion. I can't even remember the last time I'd cried that much. A ping on the computer refocused my attention on the here and now. It was Dahlia asking if I could cover the receptionist's desk so she could take a lunch break.

"Okay, Dahlia." I came up behind her at the desk. "Go take your break."

"Thanks, Lexi." She slid off the bar stool. "Do you think I can take on a client or two today?"

"I'll have a look at the schedule while you eat. I'm sure someone would be willing to let you do their nails." I looked down at my hand. "You can do mine for me."

Dahlia smiled excitedly, then turned and headed to the break room. I settled in on the bar stool and started going through the schedule for the afternoon. The bell over the door chimed. I turned to greet the customer but couldn't get the words out. Roxanne had walked into Dagger Designs. Behind her was some guy in a suit, but I didn't pay him much attention. My eyes were fixed on Roxanne.

She smiled at me. "Lexi."

"Rox." I stared dumbfounded. "You're here."

"Of course I am. I need my nails done, and Dagger Designs is the best in Frostham."

I couldn't disagree with that, but the schedule is full for the day. Dahlia could do her nails. *Will Rox remember Dahlia's work?* The salon's phone rang. It was Rita's next client. Her car broke down, and she couldn't make her scheduled appointment. She felt so bad about calling at the last minute, but I assured her it was okay and told her to call back to reschedule when she returned home.

"There's an opening." I told Rox after hanging up. "Rita should be nearly done with her current client, and then she can take you on."

"Rita." Rox said slowly. "I don't know that name."

"She was your last hire before you disappeared for two months."

"Oh." A blush tainted her cheeks, and she rubbed at her forehead. "I don't remember. I was told I was in a coma due to a car accident and may have some memory loss due to the length of time I was unconscious."

I frowned. Despite knowing the answer, I asked anyway. "Who told you all of that?"

"The doctor and my husband."

At that moment, everything Tyler told me last night struck me. Now I see that getting Roxanne back is going to be difficult. At least she remembers me, so maybe I can find out more about her current situation. Better yet, I can help her retrieve any lost memories.

Rita strolled up to the desk with Mrs. Ruth. "You have a good time on your trip, and I'll see you when you return."

"Thank you, dear." The elderly woman replied with a smile.

They both noticed Roxanne and halted. "Roxanne!"

Their exclamation was loud enough to catch the attention of everyone in the salon. Drills and fans turned off, and chatter ceased as all the attention was on the missing owner of Dagger Designs. I couldn't blame them for their reactions. If I hadn't had any prior knowledge, thanks to Tyler, I probably would have been the same way. Shocked and at a loss of words.

"Rita, your next client has cancelled. You can fill that space with Roxanne." I said, trying to remind everyone that we are at a place of business. "Mrs. Ruth, I'll ring you up."

"Yes, of course." Mrs. Ruth shook herself out of her stunned state. "I'll book my next appointment, too."

"Follow me." Rita said to Roxanne.

Rox began to follow, and the suited man she walked in with took a step forward. Rox turned and ordered him to stay where he was. With the salon's open-concept floor plan, he'd be able to see her just fine. I finished with Mrs. Ruth and realized the salon was silent.

Putting two fingers in my mouth, I whistled. "Back to work."

No one moved. They were too focused on Roxanne.

"Now!"

I swear I heard some grumbling. Slowly, the sounds of the nail salon returned. The buzz of drills and the low hum of the fans were soothing in their own strange way. The chatter between client and technician was quieter, as if they were straining to hear whatever conversation Rita and Roxanne were having.

"That was impressive."

Startled, I turned to the voice. The man who came in with Rox was staring at me with amusement in his eyes.

"What exactly are you referring to?" I questioned.

"The way you were able to get everyone to go back to work." He extended his hand. "My name is Andrew, by the way."

I eyed him suspiciously, accepting his hand not to be rude. "Lexi."

Andrew smiled, a dimple appearing on his right cheek. "That's a lovely name. Lexi. I like saying it."

"Say it too often, and you'll get bored of it." I bit out.

He laughed. "I doubt that will happen."

Is he flirting? Covertly, I scanned him from top to bottom and back up. He has sun-bleached wavy brown hair that is styled back with mousse, his brown eyes were watchful as I proceeded with my pursual, and his lips curved upward as if amused with me. He was broad-shouldered and well-built, strong-looking, and held himself with an air of superiority and military-like discipline. If I didn't have Tyler, I'd be drooling over Andrew and flirting back to get into his bed. Yet, there was something about him that put me on edge and made me weary of him.

Thankfully, I had clients coming to pay for their nails to occupy me. If I paid too much attention to Andrew, he may get the wrong idea. Dahlia returned from her lunch. Returning to her post no longer gave me an excuse to ignore Andrew.

"I'd like to take you out for dinner." Andrew propositioned.

"I think that's a wonderful idea." Rox announced, her nails now done. "Andrew can drive me home, then return to pick you up for six tonight."

"I have plans for tonight." I said, not sure if that was a lie or not.

"Another potential bad date from your dating app?" She frowned. "You deserve more. Andrew is a decent guy. Give him a chance."

My throat tightened. *She doesn't remember.* Knowing she has memory loss and experiencing it firsthand is far more painful than I anticipated. Rox clearly doesn't remember our conversation about me going after her brother, or else she wouldn't be pushing Andrew on me.

"Mrs. Frangione." Andrew interrupted. "I appreciate your aid, but I would much rather win Lexi over myself."

I frowned, not liking the idea of Andrew flirting with me more in the future.

"Dahlia." Rox smiled at the girl, then frowned. "What are you doing here?"

I put a hand up to stop Dahlia from responding. "You've been away for too long, Rox. We really need to catch up."

"That's an excellent idea. How about tomorrow?" She turned to Andrew. "That shouldn't be a problem, right?"

"You have evening plans with Mr. Frangione." Andrew reminded her. "Otherwise, your day is free for you to do as you please."

"Excellent, it's all settled." She turned back to me. "Now, how much do I owe you for today?"

"You're still the owner of Dagger Designs." I reminded her. "As long as you show up at my place tomorrow, I won't have Tyler track you down for payment."

It was meant as a joke, something she would have laughed at before the memory loss. Instead, something painful flashed in her eyes, and Andrew stiffened. He took hold of her elbow and gently tugged her away. My gut tightened. Tomorrow is going to be an important day. I will find out why the mention of her brother gives her so much pain and exactly what's missing from her memories.

Eight

TYLER

I MADE MORE PROGRESS last week working with Nico in the search for Roxanne than I did by myself using the forces' resources. If Patrick wants to put me on leave, that's fine. It'll give me more free time to find my sister. Now that she's been spotted, I'm even more motivated to bring her home.

I called Nico to let him know I was on my way to his apartment. First, though, I had to lose the tail that I spied in my rearview from my exit at the station. Whoever was tailing me was good, but I was better. Nico was waiting for me in the lobby of his apartment building when I finally parked. Visitors parked outside while there's underground parking for the residents. He raised a brow but didn't say anything until we entered his penthouse.

I looked around the modern yet comfortable-looking space. The kitchen boasted expensive name-brand appliances, which I know of because Mom coveted them when she considered renovating her kitchen. The floor-to-ceiling window in the living room provided a breathtaking view of Frostham and let in plenty of natural light.

"I expected you here sooner." Nico commented.

"I had to lose my tail." I growled, annoyed.

"Why were you tailed?"

"It probably has to do with me officially being under an IA investigation."

Nico went to the fridge, pulled out two beers, and popped the tops. "Okay, you're going to have to start at the beginning."

I took a swig of the offered beer. "I was pulled into my Captain's office first thing this morning. Mayor Jones and the Chief of Police were there."

"Patrick Mann?"

"Yeah." I said slowly, narrowing my eyes at him.

"Cazzo." He cursed.

"What's wrong?"

"He's on the Frangione payroll."

"Hell." I groaned. "That explains a lot."

He put his beer down on the breakfast bar. "Did you tell him about the doctor?"

"I did." I said, playing back to the scene in my dad's office. "The conversation started with the murder at the airstrip, which shifted onto the topic of Roxanne. Patrick used that as leverage. He was trying to push me out, so I brought up

75

the picture of her getting on a plane and the doctor. When I refused to give my leads to the officers in the missing person department, Patrick threw IA at me and demanded my badge and gun."

This day keeps getting worse. Nico pulled out his phone and made a call. He spoke urgently in Italian. The only word I picked up in the entire conversation was medico, meaning doctor. While he was on the phone, I wandered over to the window with my beer. Roxanne is out there in the city, some-where. The plane she was on with Franco would have come back by now.

"Roxanne liked that view, too." Nico stood next to me.

"She's out there."

"I know where she is."

"What?" I spun to face him. "If you know, why don't we get her back?"

Nico looked at me with a pain-filled grimace. "It'll be easier to show you."

Leaving the beer on the breakfast bar, I followed Nico to the elevator. We took it down to the parking garage, where his Mercedes-Benz was parked. It didn't surprise me that his car was a luxury vehicle — it matched his luxurious penthouse.

I slid into the passenger seat. Nico cranked the engine and floored it out of the underground parking. He kept a high speed on the roads, just below any radar setting. He drove out to Royal Heights, where the houses are massive and gated from the main road.

"What are we doing out here?" I asked, leaning forward to watch all the gates pass by.

Nico parked the car down the street and across the road from one house deep within Royal Heights. He rested his wrists on the steering wheel and leaned forward. *What makes this house special from the others?*

"Sensor plates in the wall raise the hidden barbed wire at the top. There's a security code at the gate to let people in. If you punch in the wrong code or use the code for someone already inside or who just left, security will be automatically summoned." Nico glanced over at me before returning to the house. "If you enter the code meant for guests, then you'll be greeted by Franco Frangione."

"Franco?" I looked at the gates with new interest. "Then that's where my sister is?"

"As long as she's behind that wall, in that house, you'll never get to her."

I turned to him. "You could get inside. You can get Roxanne."

Nico shook his head. "Security cameras cover every inch inside and outside the property. Only the bedrooms and bathrooms are camera-free. Those cameras are monitored twenty-four-seven by security. Each member of the security team is ex-military, highly trained, and loyal to their commander and each other."

It's a damned fortress. My mood soured, and any hope I'd felt drained instantly. "It's impenetrable."

"Pretty much." Nico agreed.

"What was the point of bringing me here?"

"So you can see where Franco is holding Roxanne." He started the car and headed back into the city. "And so you don't do something stupid, especially now that you don't have your badge."

I scowled at him. "I'm not going to leave my sister behind those gates."

"We both are until we have a plan."

I was going to comment when my phone rang. "Lexi, how has your day been?"

"She was here." Lexi whispered.

"Who was honey?" The endearment I use slipped out.

"Roxanne."

I sat up a little straighter. "Where are you? I'll come to you."

"Salon." She sounded as if holding back tears.

"I'm on my way." I hung up. "Nico, drive to Dagger Designs."

He pressed the gas a little harder. "Is Lexi okay?"

"Roxanne showed up at the salon."

Nico floored it. My head hit the backrest hard with the sudden acceleration. He has fierce determination when it comes to Roxanne. It makes him dangerous. Ironically, I trust him. Trust him to bring my sister back and keep her away from Franco.

Nico parked in the back of Dagger Designs for employees only. It was late afternoon. In a few hours, the salon would be closed, and all the staff would head home. Nico took the lead inside, flinging the doors open and storming into the office. Lexi pushed back from the desk, jumping when Nico slammed his hands on the surface. I closed the office door, sealing the three of us inside.

"Why didn't you call me?" Nico demanded. "I should have been called immediately."

"I couldn't." She said, her hands clenching the chair's arms.

"Pull back, Nico." I gripped his shoulder and physically yanked him back. "Why don't you tell us what happened, Lexi."

Lexi nodded, taking a steadying breath. "Roxanne came in like any other customer. I knew she'd have memory loss, but experiencing it was far more difficult."

"Lexi." I said softly, coming around the desk. "It will be okay."

Lexi jumped up and wrapped her arms around me, burying her face in my chest. I rubbed my hands up and down her back, holding her close. Lexi shook in my arms, trying desperately to hold back the tears I knew she wanted to shed. All I wanted to do was take her home so she could cry like she did last night.

"Nico and I will get Roxanne back." I looked over at Nico. "I promise."

"What kind of memory loss does Roxanne have?" Nico asked softly. "How much has she forgotten?"

There was so much emotion in those softly spoken words. I could see that he struggled to maintain his control and not lash out at Lexi. His emotions run hot when Roxanne's name is thrown around. I'm sure he'll cool down once she's back. I hope.

"She." Lexi sniffled, pushing back slightly but still staying within the circle of my arms. "She didn't remember Rita, the last hire she made before going missing. Rox couldn't even remember an important conversation we had."

"When was that conversation?" Nico asked.

"Um. I think it was just before you were arrested."

"Okay, so we have a baseline." I said. "What else can you tell us, Lexi?"

"I made a joke and brought up your name Tyler." Lexi looked up at me. "There was a pain-filled expression in her eyes, and her bodyguard couldn't get her out of here fast enough."

"Bodyguard?" Nico questioned.

"Someone by the name of Andrew."

There was a beat of silence before Nico let out a string of curses in Italian. He began pacing the small office between the door and the desk, looking like he wanted to throw furniture around or kill someone. I don't think I've ever seen him like this before. *Rox might be the only leash that'll be able to hold this beast back.* Nico ran his fingers through his hair, gripping the strands toward the back.

"Nico?" I asked cautiously, letting go of Lexi and coming around the desk. "Who is Andrew?"

"Head of Franco's security." Nico stopped his pacing. "Before that, he was the leader of a black ops team. Andrew is the best there is. If Franco has him on bodyguard duty, then it's going to be near impossible to get to Roxanne."

Lexi made a strangled sound. Today has been emotionally challenging for both of us. *Home, I need to get her home.*

"Near impossible." Lexi said. "That means there is a possibility."

"Yes, but the window of opportunity will be small." Nico explained.

"Lexi, why don't I take you home." I suggested.

She nodded, gathering her purse. "I will ask Rita to lock up for me."

"Are you staying the night at her place?" Nico asked when she left the office.

"That's none of your business." I snarled.

He raised his hands in surrender. "I just need to know where to have your car delivered."

"Then yes. I don't think Lexi should be alone tonight."

He nodded. When Lexi returned, we both walked her to her car. I took her keys and drove her to her apartment, then walked her upstairs.

"I'm okay, Tyler." She said when she stepped inside.

"I'm not leaving you alone." I followed her in.

"You should get home to Lucky."

I frowned at her. "He has access to the backyard, and he could learn to lose a few pounds. He's starting to get heavy to pick up."

The tiniest smile lifted the corner of her mouth before falling away. "I'm not the best company."

"Honey." I cupped her face. "I'm here for you. If all you want to do is cry while I hold you, then that's all I'll do."

Her eyes filled with tears which spilled over onto my hands. Lexi wrapped her arms around me and cried. We stood in the space between the kitchen and the living room as I held her. Eventually, Lexi's crying slowed to sniffled as she pulled back.

"I ruined your shirt." She said, placing a hand on my chest where her face was.

"It's okay." I told her. "Do you feel a little better?"

Lexi nodded, a blush creeping up her cheeks. "Could you stay the night? I just want to be held until I fall asleep."

"Anything for you."

She took my hand, leading me to her bedroom. This is the first time I've been here. The walls were a pale green, and the decorations were minimal. There was a painting and a mirror on the wall, while the bed and dresser were black and relatively modern. It's not what I pictured for Lexi, yet somehow, it fits her perfectly. My cock hardened as she began to strip out of her clothes. *Now is not the time for sex.* I settled myself on top of Lexi's pink floral duvet as she changed into an oversized nightshirt.

She slid under the covers and looked at me. "You can join me under here."

I stood, removed my shirt, jeans, and socks, and then slid under the covers with her. Lexi snuggled into my chest with a satisfied sigh. I wrapped my arm around her waist and kissed the top of her head, whispering a good night. Before long, Lexi's breathing evened out as she fell asleep.

Nine

LEXI

TYLER WAS GONE BY the time I woke up. That now makes it two times that I've broken down and cried in front of him. From my understanding, most men would panic and run as far away as possible the moment a woman tears up. Not that I had any experience in that matter. I don't show any weakness to anyone. Except for Tyler, apparently, and he didn't run. He stayed and held me as I cried.

I ran my hand over the spot in the bed Tyler had occupied last night and smiled. With Roxanne coming over today, it was probably a good thing Tyler wasn't here. After her reaction yesterday, he'd end up scaring her away. Roxanne! I kicked off the sheets, rushing through the shower so I could get dressed. She could show up at any minute. We never discussed a specific time for her to come over.

Fully dressed, I looked around my apartment. With much of my free time spent over at Tyler's house, I've been neglecting my own place. Laundry will have to wait. There's no way I'm leaving my apartment to use the building's laundry facilities. I might miss Rox's arrival. *We should have set a time.* I grabbed a broom from the tiny coat closet by the door and started with the simple chore. By the time there was a knock on the door, the surfaces were dusted, the bathroom was clean, and random items I'd left out were returned to their proper place.

"Rox!" I flung the door open excitedly, then frowned at the man who stood in the hall. "I don't recall inviting you over."

"You didn't." Andrew smiled down at me. "I would have loved one, though."

I gripped the door handle and door frame, closing the door so only my body fit in the opening. "Where's Roxanne?"

"Before I hand her over, I need to conduct a search of your apartment."

"Why?"

"To ensure Mrs. Frangione will be safe here without me."

"Rox will always be safe with me." I narrowed my eyes at him.

"Still." Andrew leaned forward. "I need to check."

There was something hard in his brown gaze. A sliver of fear ran up my spine, tightening my shoulders. Nico said Andrew was black ops before doing private security for Franco. My hands tightened, and I braced myself to keep him out in the hall.

"You are not entering my apartment." I stated.

"Lexi." Andrew reached up, running a knuckle along my cheek. "I promise to be quick."

I flinched at the contact, surprised by the zing I felt, and refused to move from my spot. "Do your search from the hall."

He frowned but didn't argue. Andrew placed one hand over mine on the door frame, and the other on the free edge of the door, then leaned in. It took a lot of willpower not to shrink away. *He's too close.* Andrew forced the door open wider so he could get a better look inside while remaining in the hall.

"Satisfied?" I asked after what felt like forever.

"Not even close, Lexi." He pulled back slowly. "It'll do for now."

Andrew stepped to the side, revealing Roxanne. The relief I felt at seeing her had me relaxing. With a smile that I missed seeing on her face, she ducked under my arm to enter my apartment. I began to close the door when Andrew placed his palm against its surface, stopping me.

"Mrs. Frangione has a dinner reservation. I'll be back later to fetch her."

With that, he left. I shut the door with a little more force than necessary. Rox's laughter was music to my ears. I turned to her, hands on my hips, glaring at her. The longer I glared, the harder she laughed. I couldn't hold the glare. A smile crept onto my lips.

"Andrew's persistent." Rox eventually wheezed out.

"Unfortunately." I grumbled, joining her in the kitchen. "How about a pizza?"

"Yum. It feels like forever since I've had one."

"Grab it from the freezer."

She spun to grab the pizza while I set the oven temperature. We moved around the kitchen like no time had passed between us as we pulled out the pizza stone and plates. Store-bought pizza never has enough goodies on it. Roxanne pulled mushrooms, a red bell pepper, and a block of cheese from the fridge. While I sliced the vegetables, Rox grated the cheese. By the time the oven was ready, we'd coated the simple pepperoni pizza and popped it inside to cook.

"While this cooks." I said, closing the oven door. "Let's move to the couch."

"Sounds good."

"So." I took hold of Rox's hands. "How are you feeling?"

Instantly, her face fell, and she blinked back tears. "Oh, Lexi. I'm so confused."

"Talk to me, Rox."

"My husband doesn't feel like my husband."

I sucked in a sharp breath. This could be good for Nico. I forced myself to collect myself. I squeezed her hands, encouraging Roxanne to continue. I don't want to scare her off. I'm all she has right now.

"When I woke up from the coma, I was disoriented." Roxanne explained. "At first, I didn't understand where I was or what had happened. I barely understood the doctor when he told me I was in a coma and that my husband was on his way. Then Franco walked in."

She stopped talking. I scooted closer, remaining silent, letting her work through whatever she was feeling.

Rox took a steadying breath before continuing. "I don't understand why I'd marry a Frangione. They killed my grandpa."

I couldn't answer that for her. Knowing Roxanne, it would have been brought up with Nico. Yet, she still fell in love with him and agreed to marry him.

"How do you feel when you're with Franco?" I asked, needing to know if there was any hope for Nico and Rox's return to the rest of us.

"Awkward." She admitted with a sheepish grin. "Franco took me away to a private island for what he called our honeymoon. There were breathtaking views, and the sex with Franco was good. I swear that man is insatiable. We christened every surface multiple times. The only time we weren't connected was when we ate."

I inwardly cringed. "But?"

"But I don't feel anything. By now, I should feel something for him, shouldn't I? He is my husband, after all."

"What do you feel when you're with Franco?"

"I feel like all I'm doing is plaything the role of a doll for Franco."

"So, no romantic feelings?" I confirmed.

Rox shook her head. "My skin crawls when he touches me casually, which I hide from him. Franco has to work to get me aroused enough for sex. Actually, having sex is the only time his touch feels good. Afterwards, I would feel sick, almost like I'm betraying someone."

The oven beeped. Just in time, too. I scurried to the kitchen not only to grab the pizza but to hide my smile. Nico will not be happy that his brother is having so much sex with his fiancée, but at least Rox has zero feelings for Franco. It's a step in the right direction. I pulled the pizza out, transferred it to a round cutting board and cut it. I collected the plates and napkins, then carried everything back to my living room. I set it on the coffee table and served up the first slice.

Roxanne was busy staring at her ring, a look of longing on her face. This gave me even more hope that Rox would overcome this memory loss. Maybe all she needs is a shock to her system, like a kiss from Nico.

"You showed me that ring when you got it." I told her, handing her a plate of food. "It might have been the happiest I've seen you. Second to you opening Dagger Designs."

"I feel happy when I look at it. The ring is gorgeous."

"You probably don't remember, but there's an inscription inside."

Roxanne accepted the pizza I offered with a frown. Placing it on her lap, she pulled off the ring. *Please work.* I mentally prayed as she read the inscription.

"Ti Amo Bella." She looked up at me. "Bella?"

I nodded. "The nickname you were given."

I'd hoped the words and the ring might help trigger some missing memories. Roxanne put the ring back on her finger and started eating. My shoulders slumped, disappointed it didn't work right away. *Maybe I pushed too hard.* I looked at Roxanne. *Maybe not.* She looked to be lost in thought.

Changing tactics, I talked about the salon, a safe topic to discuss. I caught her up on everything that she's missed. Starting with Rita, her last hire. I told her about Dahlia, reminding her that she put Dahlia through Clavus Schola, and now she's an employee. I also told her about the second Dagger Designs location. Roxanne absorbed it all, excited over the developments.

We talked for hours. For today I stayed off the topic of her family, afraid she would close up on me like she did yesterday when I mentioned Tyler. I updated her on Barbara's wedding, which made her feel horrible for making her worry. Watching Roxanne slowly make her way back to how she was before the accident was rewarding. That is until Andrew called to say he was on his way. The light she had while with me this afternoon dimmed. At least I'd made some progress. Next time, I'll bring up the subject of her family. The sooner she regains her memories, the sooner she can walk away from Franco.

Roxanne saved me from a bad relationship. It's now my chance to return the favour.

Ten

TYLER

I LEFT LEXI THIS morning so I could get a change of clothes and tend to Lucky. I wanted to go back and spend my day with her. We could talk and learn more about each other, but when I called to ask, she said she already had plans and didn't elaborate.

Lexi and I are in a relationship by title only. Nothing has really changed between us. The sex with her is fantastic, but I want more. I want her to give me her heart. The week I spent with Nico tracking down the doctor didn't help me in any way with her. It made her feel unwanted, which is not the direction I want us to be going in.

I love my sister, but I feel as though she's the reason Lexi isn't fully on board with our relationship. Until Rox is back with her family, working at Dagger Designs, and spending her nights with Nico, Lexi will never consider her own happiness. I want to be the man to make her happy. I need to figure out how to convince Lexi that not only am I the man for her but that it's okay to be happy even when there's turmoil around. *Maybe Mom will have a suggestion.*

After returning from our walk, I was filling Lucky's water bowl when my phone started to ring. "Baxter."

"It's Nico."

"Don't tell me you need me to bail you out of jail."

"I'd never stoop so low." He scoffed. "I wanted to throw a couple of plans at you and get your opinion."

I pulled the phone away and looked at the screen. *Is this a joke?* In the past two months, Nico has never run something by me. The only contact we had was when he called me to let me know of a Frangione stash house. By the time the cops showed up, everyone on site was tied up and beaten. I never revealed my source, despite department heads asking. Jaylen probably knew, but he wouldn't say anything because these busts put everyone at the station in a good mood — especially my dad.

I returned the phone to my ear. "Seriously?"

"You're not on the clock, so I thought you might want to be more involved in Roxanne's rescue." Nico said.

"Thank you." I replied. "When do you want to go over those plans?"

"Today."

"Okay. Let me get showered, and I'll meet you at your place."

He confirmed that it would work and hung up on me. I showered and dressed and then went over to Nico's. He wasn't in the lobby to meet me. This time, he texted me a guest code for me to enter the building on my own. I rode the elevator up to Nico's penthouse and knocked on the door.

"Good, you're here." Nico greeted.

I stepped into his home, keeping an eye on him as he returned to the depths of his place. He looked even worse than when I last saw him yesterday. I closed and locked the door before following him. The dining table was covered with a map of Frostham and all sorts of loose papers while his laptop and phone were sitting open on a corner of the table.

"What is all of this?" I asked.

Picking up a paper with information on Obsidian, a club he owned before Franco took it over, and reviewed the information. This was the entire catalyst for Roxanne's car accident. Nico's name was still on the ownership. Jaylen and I arrested him, accusing him of all sorts of crimes that were linked to the club. Determined to prove that Nico was innocent, Roxanne went to Franco, who blackmailed her for a date at the mayor's auction, a fundraiser for the city. It was that night that she was in the car accident and kidnapped.

"Everything I've been able to collect on Franco and his businesses from the last two months." Nico answered.

"Why?"

"He took what was important to me. I'm going to take the empire he's so proud of."

I put the paper down and looked at him. "Have you showered or eaten? You don't even look like you've slept."

"I'll get around to it."

"Go shower, shave and put some clean clothes on." I ordered. "I'll scrounge around your kitchen and make you something to eat."

Nico glared at me. "Not necessary. Let's get to work."

"It's necessary." I crossed my arms, challenging him. "You smell and look like a homeless person. Feeling and looking more like yourself will help settle your mind. While food will help you focus."

"Tyler." He growled. "Now is not the time for luxuries."

I blinked, a little surprised that he'd called me by name for the first time. "Now is the perfect time. Roxanne is in the city. You wouldn't want her to see you in this state, even if it's from afar."

Nico grumbled something Italian under his breath and stomped off. I couldn't help the satisfied grin on my face. My sister really is the best bribe or blackmail piece to keep Nico Frangione in line. Opening the fridge, I spied ingredients for an omelette. It would be filling and nutritious to keep him going for the day. Since I'm making one for Nico, I might as well make one for myself.

Nico returned looking much better. There were still bags under his eyes, but at least he looked presentable. I placed an omelette on the breakfast bar. He eyed it, but the loud growl of his stomach settled the argument of whether or not he should eat.

"While you eat." I said, breaking into my omelette. "Talk to me about your plans."

"Okay." Nico said a little too enthusiastically. "I've been thinking about it, and there are only two ways to free Roxanne from Franco's clutches."

"Which are?"

"We launch an attack and kidnap her while Andrew is the only protection she has. Or we destroy Franco's empire, which will force him, Andrew and the rest of his security to investigate, which will leave Roxanne alone and unprotected."

"Based on what you told me yesterday about Andrew, the security team, and the fortress Franco calls a home, I see too many flaws in both of those plans."

"Obviously, there are some kinks that need to be ironed out."

I sighed. "I want my sister back as much as you do."

Nico growled, not entirely agreeing with my statement.

"But I'm not willing to put Rox's life in danger in any way during her rescue." I continued, ignoring him. "Finish eating, and then we can explore both options in detail."

Nico and I spent hours going over every possible scenario we could come up with. Destroying Franco's empire would require an army, and since I don't have a badge anymore, it would be a challenge to complete. In theory, Nico could recruit the manpower, but it could also backfire and put him in a jail cell with no bail. Or it could start a war on the streets, and innocent Frostham residents could be caught in the crossfire. This route could potentially put Franco on high alert and go underground with Roxanne.

Kidnapping my sister while Andrew is her only protection is more plausible, except we don't know when or where she'll be for us to execute any plan. We'd most likely need a couple of extra bodies to help us, which would be easy enough, but we can't make a solid plan. If we followed them around waiting for an opportunity, then Andrew would probably spot us and be on high alert. If we can figure out the best time, date, or place to execute the kidnapping, then there'd be less chance of Andrew getting in our way.

"Face it, Nico." I sat back in the dining chair and ran my hand over my face. "We need an inside man. Except we can't do that because none of Franco's people will turn on him, and if we send someone in, then Franco and Andrew will be suspicious."

"There has to be a way." Nico pushed away from the table and went to the kitchen. "Do you want a water?"

"I'm good. I should be heading out soon."

Nico's phone began to ring. I looked over at the caller ID.

"Who is 'Loyal Guard Dog'?"

Nico rushed to answer the phone. "Are you okay?"

I raised a brow at his concern over whoever was on the other end. Clearly, it was someone he cared about. Whatever answer he was given, Nico's shoulders had relaxed.

"Yes, I'm free to talk right now." Nico answered the other person. "Are you sure?" His brows knitted, and the concern was returning to his face. "Very well, we'll talk tomorrow."

"Is everything okay?" I asked when he hung up.

"I'm not entirely sure."

"Anything I can do to help?"

"No, not tonight." Nico looked over at me. "Shouldn't you be making your way to your parents' house? It is Sunday, after all, Tyler."

I frowned at him. There was nothing more I could say. Nico looked like he needed time to think something over. As long as he doesn't get arrested, he can do whatever he wants. *I hope he doesn't make a move without me.*

I drove over to my parents' house, mulling over all the information I'd absorbed tonight. Apparently, all the arrests made in the past two months were small fry in Franco's empire. Except, none of it actually connected to Franco. From what I gathered today, if Franco continues to succeed and grow his empire, he'll be even more powerful than Enzo. He could absorb all of his father's business and become untouchable in the criminal world.

"Hi, Mom." I called out upon entering their home.

"I'm in the kitchen, Tyler." She called back.

I joined her. "Is Dad not back from work yet?"

She stopped what she was doing to hug me. "He called to say he's running behind but should be arriving in about fifteen minutes. How have you been?"

I shrugged. "I've been put on immediate leave pending an internal affairs investigation."

"What? Why?"

"Patrick Mann thinks I'm spending too much time looking for my sister and not enough time on my job."

"That insufferable man." She grumbled. "What did your father say?"

"Nothing." I said, feeling a little bitter.

"I'll talk with him."

"Don't, Mom. I've already told him that his hatred is going to cost him."

Mom smiled. "That's my boy. Now, come mash these potatoes while I make gravy for the chicken."

I kissed her cheek before obeying the command. I knew she'd understand.

"I'd like your advice on something." I hedged.

"About what?"

"A woman."

Mom stopped stirring the gravy to look at me, her eyes wide. "I didn't know you were dating someone."

"It's sort of new." I admitted. "We're in a relationship, but I feel like she's holding back."

"Have you talked to her about it?" She resumed her stirring. "That would be the first step."

"Not directly, but I have a suspicion on where the conversation will go."

"Oh? You know her that well already?"

"I doubt she'll say it out loud, but I fear she doesn't believe she deserves to be happy when someone she knows isn't happy." I explained vaguely. "What advice can you give me so I can convince her that she deserves to be happy."

"Talk to her." Mom repeated. "There could be some other cause that's impeding her growth in the relationship with you. Start there."

Not the answer I was hoping for, but I thanked her and kissed her cheek. Dad walked in with Jaylen. He's become a fixture at our family dinners. The tension between Dad and me was palatable, and I was going to make it worse. Partway through the meal, I announced to everyone about Rox's visit to Dagger Designs. Dad caused a scene, telling me that I was putting my career in jeopardy, while Mom teared up. I didn't mention anything about the rescue plans Nico and I are trying to make. They'll know when I return home with Roxanne.

Eleven

LEXI

"KNOCK, KNOCK."

I looked up from payroll and smiled. "Roxanne. This is a wonderful surprise."

"Well, after our talk yesterday about the salon, it hit me how much I missed it." She grinned.

"And we've all missed you."

"Franco being insatiable has an upside. It took me all night to convince him to let me come back to work."

I frowned. "Why would you need to bribe your husband to let you do something?"

"He's afraid a business rival will use me to get to him. Franco would prefer I stay at home."

"That's no way to live, Rox."

"The sex might only be good, but Franco is creative in how he claims me."

There was so much wrong in those few sentences. Yet, my mind conjured a few ideas about how creative one could be in bed, with Tyler as the male lead, of course. I almost asked Roxanne for details for my own personal use, but then I decided against it. This marriage she has with Franco is a shame, and I don't want to encourage it in any way.

"So you're back full-time?" I asked.

"Three days a week."

I grimaced. "Better than nothing."

"It's the best I could get." She shrugged. "Franco only wanted me to work two days a week."

"I'll take it." I said. "I need to make a trip to the second Dagger Designs location. Would you like to join me?"

"Yes." Roxanne clapped her hands excitedly. "I can't wait."

I smiled at her. "Let me finish payroll for this employee, then we can go."

"I'll let Andrew know."

She turned on her heels and left me to finish the work. Before leaving the office, I shot Nico a quick text, rescheduling our lunch for an after-work meet-up. There is no way I'm going to miss this precious time with Roxanne. *He'll understand.* When I went out front, to where I assumed Rox was waiting, I found her in Candi's embrace.

"I'm so happy to see you." Candi said, pushing her back to arm's length. "Where have you been?"

I stepped up to Roxanne while addressing the brunette. "Now's not a good time to catch up, Candi."

"Right, I'm sure you're busy catching up with everyone after such a long time away."

"Where I've been is none of your business, Princess." Rox interjected while crossing her arms.

Silence fell between the three of us. I stared dumbfounded at my best friend. Candi, on the other hand, began to laugh.

"What's so funny?" Rox narrowed her eyes.

"I didn't realize how much I'd missed that nickname." Candi explained.

"Where's Brina? Aren't you two influencers glued to the hip?"

Candi frowned. "She's living in an influencer house in Alexo."

"Oh."

"Candi, I'm ready for you." Rita joined the small group.

"Yes, I'm coming." Candi nodded, reaching out to squeeze Rox's wrist. "We can talk later."

As Candi started to walk past and into the salon, I grabbed her forearm and leaned in to whisper. "If you can, visit Franco tonight."

She nodded slowly, her eyes flickering to Roxanne. Candi might become a helpful ally in retrieving Rox's memories, or she could help to lure Rox away from Franco without drawing any suspicion from him.

Andrew was out front waiting for us. The back door to the sedan was open for us to slide in. I would have preferred to drive myself and leave this man behind, but unfortunately, he's a packaged deal with Roxanne for now. Before sliding in, I provided the address of the second location.

Roxanne, looking pensive, shifted in her seat to stare at me. "I've called Candi 'Princess' before?"

"It started the first time she walked into Dagger Designs." I said, hoping she could fill in some of the blanks herself.

"Throwing a fit." Roxanne said slowly while rubbing her forehead. "Brina was with her. Candi wanted us to fix the nails she had done at another salon."

I held my breath. That was also the day she met Nico.

"There was someone else there, a shadow. Maybe her bodyguard." She threw her head back onto the headrest with a frustrated grunt. "Everything around Candi is a blur. I can't remember."

"It'll come." I squeezed her knee. "Those memories won't stay locked away forever."

Roxanne unconsciously spun her wedding ring around her finger. The memory might not surface if she focuses too much on it, so I told her more about the second salon. The hired construction crew finished the inside of the space that Roxanne picked out before her car accident right on schedule. I didn't tell her that Nico had paid for the crew. It wouldn't have mattered if she couldn't remember him. The salon was nearly a replica of the first location. Two weeks ago, there was a soft opening, letting our clients know through a newsletter so that the staff could be assessed before a grand opening for the rest of Frostham.

Andrew parked in the salon's shared parking lot with a handful of other businesses. He opened the back door and helped us out of the car. I took in the outside façade with a frown.

"This isn't how I left it." I said.

The front windows were dirty, and the custom decals could barely be seen. As we neared, a short woman with long black hair braided and resting over her shoulder came out of the salon. She put down a bucket that she'd brought outside with her.

"Rossalyn." I called out.

She turned with a smile. "Lexi."

"What happened to the salon?"

"Hoodlums."

"Let me clean these windows. You ladies, go inside." Andrew said.

He removed his suit jacket and handed it to Roxanne. He then rolled up his sleeves and dipped his hands into the bucket. On his inner arm was a tattoo, but I couldn't see it clearly. Andrew pulled out a wet cloth and began washing the windows. I pulled the door open for Rossalyn and Rox to enter.

"What the —?" I couldn't believe my eyes. "Rossalyn what happened?"

"Someone broke in last night." She said in a way of explanation.

"Did you call the cops?"

"Two officers took statements and a copy of the security feed."

Roxanne grimaced. "Those officers aren't going to do anything."

"I agree." Rossalyn said.

On the floor, someone painted a beautiful sunset at a lake. Phrases like "This is Real Art" and "Posers" were painted crudely both on the floor and the walls. Glitter, dip powder, and other nail accessories from the display wall were scattered all over the floor. *Why would anyone do this?*

"We had to call all of our clients and reschedule them." Rossalyn explained. "I didn't want anyone seeing this."

"You should have called me." I stated.

"I wanted to handle this myself."

"I'm calling Franco." Roxanne announced. "He can send in a professional cleaning crew."

"No." I said, not wanting Franco involved with Dagger Designs in any way. "I know a crew that can come in tonight, maybe even sooner. By the time they are done, no one, except us, will know what's occurred."

She nodded reluctantly. Belatedly, I introduced Roxanne to Rossalyn and asked her to introduce the employees from this location that were busy trying to clean up the mess. I went to the back office to make a phone call to Nico.

"Hey." He said softly. "You cancelled on me."

"Postponed." I corrected. "And you'll be happy I did."

"Oh?"

"I'm calling because I made a trip out to the second salon location." I logged onto the computer to watch the security feed. "Someone broke in and vandalized the place."

"Vandalized how?"

"Painted the floor and walls. Destroyed some supplies. Thankfully, nothing that can't be easily replaced."

"Cops?" He asked.

"Called but useless. The manager here called it in before I arrived."

Nico laughed. "Of course. I'm surprised you didn't call Tyler about this."

"Can you send a crew to clean up the mess?" I asked, hopeful. "I'd like to reopen for clients tomorrow without a speck of evidence of the vandalism."

"When do you want the crew there?"

"As soon as possible."

"I'll let you know when they are on their way over."

He hung up after I thanked him. I owe Nico a lot for his help. Updating him on Rox's memory condition might be enough to cover the clean-up crew.

Twelve

TYLER

I met with Jaylen for lunch at Malley's, a sports pub with the best burgers in the city. It was a little risky meeting him here since it's a popular spot for our fellow officers to have a quick bite. Knowing their clientele, Malley's has a quick-order menu that can have a meal ready within five, maybe ten, minutes of ordering. The bill is placed on the table immediately for a quick escape. Since I'm no longer on the clock, I can savour a bacon cheeseburger this time.

"Are you sure this is a good idea?" Jaylen questioned me when he slid into the booth I occupied. "We could have had lunch anywhere."

I shrugged. "We're two friends having lunch, that's all."

My partner frowned. "How have you been without your badge?"

"I'll get it back."

"Detectives." A cute strawberry-blonde waitress sidled up to the booth. "What can I get you today?"

"Peppercorn bacon cheeseburger." I said, sliding her the menu I had been given when I sat down. "With a side of gravy for the fries."

"Sure thing." She jotted down my order and then turned her attention to Jaylen. "What can I get you, Detective?"

"Club sandwich, and I'll have onion rings instead of the fries." Jaylen ordered without looking at the menu.

"Coming right up. Will you be needing the receipt immediately?"

"I'll cover his lunch." I told the waitress. "No rush on the bill."

She nodded and left. I swear her shoulders sagged when I answered instead of Jaylen. My partner didn't even give her a second look. Instead, he glared at me.

"What?"

"Just because you're buying my lunch doesn't mean I'm going to tell you anything." He told me.

I shrugged. "That's fine."

Jaylen snorted. "I don't believe that."

"I don't need to know what's happening at the station." I lied.

The waitress returned with two glasses of coke and told us she'd return shortly with our food. Both items are on the quick-order menu. When the burger was in front of me, I leaned in to take a long inhale of the delicious smell. This is a treat, being able to savour the food instead of only devouring it.

"Enjoy." The waitress smiled, subtly leaning toward Jaylen. "Let me know if there's anything else I can get you."

"Thanks." Jaylen smiled at her.

She sucked in a breath, swooning slightly. There was a crash somewhere in the restaurant, breaking this waitress's spell. She jumped, turning to search the restaurant for the source before walking away.

"She likes you." I stated while dipping a fry in the gravy ramekin.

"I'm not interested." Jaylen grumbled.

"I'm not saying you should take her on a date, but she might be fun in bed."

"Still not interested." He bit into his club viciously.

I let out a sigh. "You're never going to get over Roxanne if you don't try meeting someone else."

"What about you?" Jaylen snapped. "You haven't been with anyone in three years, not since that blonde at the bar."

I couldn't help the smile that grew on my face. "She's back in my bed."

He blinked. "When did that happen?"

"Recently." I hunched over to take a big bite of burger.

"Will I officially get to meet this woman?"

"Yes."

"When?"

"Eventually."

Technically, you've already met. My partner frowned at my short one-word answers. If I had my way, I'd be showing Lexi off as my girlfriend to anyone who'll listen. *I need to talk to her about that.* We haven't put a title on our relationship, and I want that. I want to solidify what we are to one another. Maybe it'll help her move forward.

We fell silent as we continued to eat. Jaylen scarfed down his food, glancing at his watch periodically. His plate was empty by the time I'd finished my burger. He pushed his plate to the free edge of the table and stared at me. I held his gaze as I dipped my fries into the gravy and continued to eat my lunch.

"Forensics confirmed it was cigar ash at the airstrip." Jaylen said quietly.

"The same kind found in Rox's car?"

He nodded. A growl of frustration rumbled free. We never could find the owner of that cigar, which indicates that we'll never find the airstrip killer. Or rather, Jaylen will never find him since I'm technically on leave. A small part of me was thrilled that, in a roundabout way, it proved Nico's innocence.

"I have to get back to the station." Jaylen slid out of the booth. "Thanks for lunch, Ty."

"Be careful." I said. "Patrick Mann is on the Frangione payroll."

His features darkened. Nodding his understanding, he left the restaurant. The strawberry-blonde waitress came by to clear the empty plates and give me the bill. I studied it while she went to fetch the machine. While I paid, I caught her looking longingly at the seat Jaylen previously occupied. *She must have it bad.*

"Thank you." I smiled when I handed back the machine.

"You're welcome, Detective." She smiled back politely.

"Tyler, and my partner's name is Jaylen."

She nodded, her smile widening. "Have a good day, Tyler."

"You too."

"Oh." Her cheeks tinted in embarrassment. "My name is Amanda."

She's been serving us for the past couple of years, but I think that's the first time I've heard her name. Amanda may have introduced herself the first few times we came here, as all waitresses do, but clearly, neither Jaylen nor I paid much attention. From what I know now, it would have been because he was with my sister, and I've never forgotten my night with Lexi.

Maybe I should stop by to see her. Thrilled with the idea, I made my way to Dagger Designs. I greeted Rita at the reception desk and walked to the back, only to frown at the empty office. Memories of my sister at that desk, smiling whenever I stopped by, filled my mind. With the room empty, those memories hurt. Presenting my back to the empty office, I pulled out my phone to call Lexi.

"Hello?" She answered.

"Lexi, it's Tyler."

"Hey." Her voice softened. "Sorry, I didn't check caller ID before picking up."

"Is everything okay?"

"No." She grumbled. "If I were to send you a video, do you think you could track down a couple of people?"

"If facial recognition can identify them, then sure." I said.

"Never mind then."

"Where are you right now?"

"At the salon."

She couldn't see it, but my frown deepened. "Is there some hidden room that I don't know about?"

Lexi went silent a moment before she chuckled. "The second location."

"Right. I'll be over shortly."

"No!" She exclaimed. "No, there's really no need. I'm quite busy over here."

She was hiding something from me. The question is, what?

"Then let me help lighten the load." I pushed.

"I'm good. Everything is covered."

"Lexi, honey."

My words were cut off when another male voice spoke. He was close enough to her that I could hear him clearly through the phone.

"Lexi, the windows are clean. What else can I do to help?"

"Give me a second." Lexi then said to me. "I have to go, bye."

She hung up. I stared down at my phone. *Who the hell was that?* This guy was allowed to help, but I wasn't. A terrible scenario popped into my head, and I had to swallow down my anger. Maybe she's getting tired of me, and this guy is her next bedmate. I shook my head, even thinking the scenario sounded ridiculous, yet I couldn't stop the anger at the very idea of it.

Needing answers, I drove to the other salon. This one is a stand-alone building in a busy area with a grocery store, a restaurant, and other businesses. I parked at a distance in the shared parking lot and kept my eyes on the door. With the decals covering the windows, I couldn't see inside, but I could clearly see the closed sign on the door.

Arguing with myself about the pros and cons of showing up uninvited, I stayed in the car. *I trust Lexi, but I need to know.* Finally, an hour later, deciding that I'd be able to kiss away any anger Lexi might have over my impromptu visit, I opened the car door to get out, then froze. Lexi stepped out of the salon with another woman, a man in a suit, and Roxanne. I stared dumbly at my sister. Lexi was with Roxanne and didn't tell me.

I closed the car door and stared at the man through the windshield window. That had to be Andrew. As if he sensed my stare, he looked over in my direction. The hairs on the back of my neck stood on end. I wasn't sure if he saw me or was only searching the general area. It didn't matter. I could sense the dangerous aura wafting off of him from this distance.

Two panel vans pulled up to the salon, and a bunch of men got out. Lexi stepped closer to one of them, handed him a key and spoke to him for a moment. The men gathered supplies from the vans and entered the salon. Lexi turned to Andrew. He stood at a black sedan, the back door open as he waited for her.

I followed the car back to the original Dagger Designs. Andrew parked the car in the back and helped Lexi out of the car. She pulled away from him right away, but he crowded her

113

and shuffled her into a blind spot from where I had parked. I saw red. Andrew and Lexi were hidden from my view for much longer than I deemed appropriate. Finally, Andrew slid back into his car and drove off with Roxanne. As much as I wanted to follow my little sister, I wanted answers from Lexi much more.

I followed Lexi from Dagger Designs to Luxlia, Nico's luxury car dealership. She got out of her car and waited by the front door. Two minutes later, Nico pulled up, and she got in. *What is going on?* Not only is Lexi keeping Roxanne, and who knows what other secrets, from me, but she's also confiding in Nico instead of me.

Frustrated, I went home. Lucky greeted me with his usual enthusiasm. Needing to clear my mind, I hooked up my dog to his leash and took him for a walk.

Thirteen

LEXI

AFTER TYLER'S PHONE CALL, I felt even more guilty about keeping Roxanne away from him — both yesterday and today. But I had to. The way Andrew rushed her away the other day, I just knew that if Tyler showed up, Rox would be taken away, and I may not see her again. It didn't matter how much sex she'd have with Franco. He'll keep her away from her family no matter what.

Rossalyn, Roxanne, Andrew, and I spent a few hours cleaning up the salon's mess. I did whatever I could to ease Nico's cleaning crew's work. The employees who had come in were sent home. They weren't going to get any work done anyway.

Nico texted me to let me know the cleaning crew was close. That was our cue to head out. I handed the key to the same man who helped get the salon ready for opening, asking him to lock up when he was done. Then Andrew drove me back to Dagger Designs.

"Lexi." Andrew helped me out of the car. "Let me follow you home."

"Not necessary." I pulled away at the soonest opportunity.

He shuffled me toward my car. "We've had a tail since leaving the salon. I want to ensure you get home safely."

"I will be fine."

Andrew put a hand on my car door, preventing me from making my escape. He leaned in, and I leaned back.

"What are you doing?" I demanded.

"This." Andrew said.

He cupped my cheek and brushed his lips against mine. They tingled at the contact. Then he pressed forward and kissed me. My eyes widened in shock and I gasped. *What the hell?* Andrew deepened the kiss by sweeping his tongue inside, then pulled back.

"Stay safe." He smiled at me, pecking my lips before walking away.

I reached up and touched my lips. They still tingled from the contact. My brain had fried when he kissed me, too stunned to react sensibly. *I should have slapped him.* Andrew was almost back in his car when proper sense returned to me. I frantically wiped at my mouth and spat on the ground.

"Disgusting." I mumbled, pulling out my phone and getting into my car.

"Lexi." Nico answered when I called. "Is it time?"

"I'm on my way to Luxlia."

"I'll be waiting."

I made my way to his place of business. Parking my car, I got out and waited for Nico. I didn't have to wait long before he pulled up for me to get in. I didn't say anything, and neither did he as he drove around Frostham. *This is going to be difficult.*

"Roxanne was at my apartment yesterday." I told him, lowering my gaze to my hands, which were twisting in my lap. "We talked for hours."

"Is that why you called me yesterday?" He asked, glancing over. "Can you tell me what you talked about?"

"We mostly talked about the salon." I swallowed. "I learnt something."

"What did you learn, Lexi?"

"You're not going to like it."

"Tell me."

I took a deep breath, letting it out slowly. "Roxanne believes she's married to Franco and they've been having constant sex."

"What!"

Nico slammed on the brakes. The cars behind him honked their annoyance. Thank goodness he didn't cause an accident, but he could have. The sudden motion had me lurching forward against the seat belt. *I should have waited to tell him at a red light.*

"Sorry." Nico mumbled.

He steered the car off the road, parked it at a strip mall, and sat there, his hands white-knuckling the steering wheel. I didn't dare say anything. I suspected this is how he'd react to the news.

"I knew she was told that she was married to Franco." Nico said through clenched teeth. "But the sex. How could she fall into bed with him?"

"Waking disoriented from a coma, then being told her husband is on his way, and then having Franco walk in." I defended my best friend. "I'd say it was too easy for her to be manipulated, and sex is the best way to do that."

"Cazzo!" He slammed his hands on the steering wheel three times before running his fingers through his hair. "Quell maledetto batardo. Lo scuoierò vivo e poi lo ucciderò."

I had no idea what he said. Based on the venom in his voice, I'd wager it had something to do with a vow to kill Franco.

"There's hope, Nico." I said softly, lightly touching his arm. "She knows something is wrong. She told me she feels like a doll playing a role when she's with Franco."

"Really?"

I smiled and snagged his hand with his engagement ring. "Her ring, the ring you got her, she still has it, and it makes her happy."

A hopeful yet sad smile curved his lips. "Thanks, Lexi, I needed that."

"I have a little more good news."

"Oh?"

"She'll be working with me at Dagger Designs three days a week."

"I could kiss you." Nico stated as a genuine smile blossomed on his face. "That's excellent news. How did you manage it?"

"I didn't." I told him, frowning. "Rox came to me today with that announcement. She said after our talk yesterday, she missed the salon and convinced Franco to let her work."

A dark scowl and a matching growl turned Nico into a very dangerous man. It made me very happy that I was on his good side. He had the same dangerous look when Roxanne was taken, or so I was told by Tyler. Fully prepared to burn the world down to get her back. When he failed in the first month, he became like a wounded animal, but he was back with a vengeance. The saying hell has no fury, like a woman scorned, is nothing compared to Nico Frangione on the path to rescue his fiancée.

Nico put the car in drive and returned to Luxlia. I opened the door to get out when Nico grabbed my wrist.

"I will bring Roxanne back to us. I promise."

I smiled at him. "All the princess needs is a kiss from her prince charming."

That caused him to laugh, and his shoulders relaxed. I was nearly home when I remembered that I had forgotten to tell him about Candi's visit to the salon and Rox's memory of their first encounter. *Note to self: call Nico.* Coming out of the elevator of my apartment building, I stumbled over my feet. Tyler was sitting on the floor outside my door with Lucky in his lap.

"Tyler? What are you doing here?"

"I wanted to see you." He said, looking up at me.

My heart leapt up to my throat. I don't know how long those words, words I crave to hear, will be said. Eventually, Tyler will get bored of me and move on. My heart plummeted down to my stomach. *No. I can't let my fear take hold.* Stepping over his outstretched legs, I unlocked my apartment door. Tyler pushed himself off the ground with one hand and then proceeded to follow me inside.

"Tyler, I'm tired. It's been a long day." I placed my purse on the kitchen counter and turned to him. "If you're here for sex, I'm going to have to decline."

He'd locked the door and put Lucky down, who immediately began to wander the new space. "That's not why I came, Lexi."

"It's not?"

"No." Tyler growled, planting fists on his hips. "Do I look like a sex-only kind of man?"

Purposefully, slowly, I scanned his length. My eyes met his before answering. "Yes."

"Well, when I asked you for a relationship, I wanted more than sex."

"That's all we've done." I said. "Except those two nights where all I've done is cry."

"That is going to change." Tyler's annoyed expression softened, and he closed the distance between us. "I want to take you out on dates. I want to get to know everything about you, learn all your quirks, and be able to predict your mood with a glance. I want your trust, and your love, and your heart."

I shook my head. *This has to be a dream.* Pretty words to keep me in his bed. Though, I wish they were all true. I want all the same things from Tyler that he wants from me.

"I want to tell people that you're my girlfriend." He said.

That word. My whole body stiffened, and my stomach began to churn. Use that word to describe anyone else's relationship, and I'm fine. When used to describe me in a relationship, it makes me sick.

"Lexi?" Tyler asked, his brows knitting. "Are you okay?"

I couldn't answer him. All the air was sucked out of my lungs with that one word. Turning, I raced to the bathroom, falling to my knees in front of the toilet seconds before I threw up. There wasn't much in my stomach. After the initial bout of stomach acid and my lunch, I proceeded to dry heave.

To my utter embarrassment, Tyler had followed and held my hair back. When my stomach settled and the toilet was flushed, I still sat there on the floor just in case. Tyler ran the water at the sink, returning to my side and lifting my face so he could wipe it clean with a cloth.

"What happened?" He asked softly.

"That word." I replied when I thought it was safe.

"What word?"

He took a moment to think, then started to say it. I slapped my hands over his mouth.

"Don't." I pleaded. "Please don't say it or call me by it."

Tyler pulled my hands away and settled himself on the floor. "Okay."

"Thank you."

Lucky came into the bathroom. I reached out to scratch his head. The dog settled his head on my knee as if sensing I needed comfort.

"Will you tell me what happened to give you such a visceral reaction to a single word?" Tyler asked, keeping his tone soft.

I don't really want to tell him. If he learns the story, he may walk away. I am damaged goods, after all, in the serious relationship department. Then, a tiny voice in the back of my mind was reminding me that he was the one. If it's true, he'll understand, he'll stay. Tyler is different. *I need to trust him.*

I took a steadying breath and dragged Lucky into my lap. "Do you know how Rox and I became friends?"

"You two took the same business course at college, right?"

"That's how we met." I confirmed. "It was because of her curious and nosy personality that we became friends. If it weren't for Rox, I wouldn't be here."

"What does that even mean?" He asked.

I held Lucky closer to my chest. I've never repeated this story before, except for Roxanne. She never expressed any pity for me, only anger at how I was being used. It endeared me to her. She saved me.

"The boy I was dating in my last year of high school was really sweet and thoughtful. I fell for him hard and fast. Then, in college, I gave myself to him." I kept my gaze anywhere but on Tyler. "Shortly after, he began to change."

Tyler sucked in a breath. I didn't see, but I could sense his muscles tense. Thankfully, he didn't say anything as I struggled to find the words to continue.

"His sweet demeanour slowly transitioned. I was wrapped up with him after being his... his girlfriend." I choked on the word. "For a long time. I was convinced that despite how he treated me, I should still support him and do everything I could to keep him happy."

"Lexi." He said, lightly cupping my cheek.

I leaned into his touch, finding comfort in the simple gesture. "Then I met Roxanne. She took it upon herself to befriend me and insert herself into my life."

Tyler chuckled. "That sounds like my sister."

"She showed me what a healthy, loving relationship should be like. I began to desire what Jenna and Herald have, your parents were my inspiration for my future. With Rox at my back, I broke up with my boyfriend."

"Good."

"That word still brings back all the bad memories." I told him. "I stuck with dating apps to try and find that one person who could treat me right. I thought I found it with you, then you left me hanging that one week, and I began to question our relationship."

"I'm sorry."

"I don't want to fall into another bad relationship Tyler. I'm hesitant to move forward because I'm afraid you're an illusion, and eventually, you'll get tired of me and move on. I don't want to be hurt by you, yet I can't bring myself to let you go."

"Lexi, I'm no illusion. I'm the real deal."

Tyler began leaning in, his hand on my cheek travelling to the back of my neck. I sucked in a breath, both in anticipation and shock. I want his lips on mine, yet I can't quite believe he still wants to kiss me after everything I just said. Lucky, forgotten during my recollection, wiggled in my arms so he could better lick my face. I let out a laugh and continued to laugh as Lucky continued his licks.

"Okay, Lucky." Tyler took the dog from my lap and rubbed his belly. "Way to take my thunder."

The beagle barked and licked at his owner's face. Tyler appeased the dog for a few licks before setting him on the bathroom floor. He then stood and helped me up. Tyler took me to the bedroom and laid me on the mattress.

"That jerk you dated, he never deserved you." Tyler said, crawling on top of me. "You may have horrible flashbacks with the g-word. But make no mistake, Lexi Dawson, you are my woman."

"I am?"

He stared down at me, a very serious expression on his face. "Yes, honey, you are my woman."

Fourteen

TYLER

I'VE THOUGHT THIS BEFORE, and I'll think it again: waking up with Lexi in my arms is heaven. Last night, I got an insight into Lexi Dawson. Giving her an option while in a relationship makes her hesitate. The jerk she dated in college did a number on her. Because of him, she's now hesitant about any future relationship. Though I am going to be the last relationship she's ever going to need. I told her decisively that she was mine, then proceeded to show her with my body that I would never get tired of her. Mom was right. Talking with Lexi showed me what was impeding her from going all out in our relationship.

Lexi turned, curling into my side and let out a contented little sigh. I smiled at her, my fingers tenderly tracing the length of her spine. A pleasurable little moan rumbled through her frame, and she stretched her gorgeously naked body along mine.

"Morning." Lexi murmured, flinging a leg over mine and resting her chin on my chest.

"Morning." I leaned down to kiss her.

Lexi smiled into the kiss. Her hand travelled down and wrapped around my cock. "More like morning wood."

"Lexi." I groaned.

With a mischievous grin, she shimmied down my body and sucked my cock into her mouth. *God, that feels good.* Lexi's blue eyes sparkled as she worked. Lost in the feeling of Lexi's mouth and hands on me, I twisted my fingers in her hair and held her still as I thrust deep and ejaculated. It took me a minute to realize what I'd done, and I pulled Lexi off my cock.

"I'm sorry." I sat up, her face cupped in my hands. "I am so sorry, Lexi."

"Tyler." She cupped my face in return. "No apology needed."

"But, I shouldn't have —."

I began to explain when Lexi kissed me. I could taste myself on her lips. It was oddly erotic.

"If I wasn't willing to swallow, I would have bit down on your cock or dug my nails into your balls." Lexi stated, a blush creeping up her neck. "I, uh, haven't done that since college. Was it any good?"

"Mind-blowing." I assured her. "Now, let me return the favour."

Music began playing in the room. "My alarm. I have to get ready for work."

"You can be a little late." I pushed her onto her back and ran my tongue along the seam of her entrance. "Let me taste you."

She moaned, her hips arching in a silent plea. "Tyler, I'll be late."

"You own the salon." I sucked on her clit, nipping it lightly.

"That's not an excuse." Her breathing was ragged.

I took my time dipping my tongue between her folds, getting a good taste of her before bringing my head up and closing her legs. "I wouldn't want you to be late because of me."

Lexi stared at me wide-eyed and slack-jawed. I pulled her up for a kiss, murmuring that we should take a shower. While under the hot spray of the small shower, I used my hand to bring Lexi to the orgasm that was building while on her bed. Finally cleaned and dressed, we left her apartment together. Lexi went to work, and I returned home with Lucky.

My dog went straight to his food dish and whined. I winced. Staying over at Lexi's was impromptu, and she didn't have any dog stuff in her apartment. As I filled his dish with food, I made a mental note to make a care pack to leave in my car for when these occasions happen again. Or better yet, I should have Lexi move in with me.

I sat on the kitchen floor, petting Lucky as he ate. "I'm sorry about last night, bud. I got swept up in all things Lexi."

He raised his head to bark at me. I wasn't sure if he was agreeing with me or complaining about it. Either way, I have to be more mindful. I can't ignore my dog because of a woman.

"Yeah, she's easy to get swept up with." I frowned, thinking of the conversation we had yesterday. "I never knew Lexi had such an unhealthy relationship. One would never know. She's such a strong, independent woman. So beautiful and caring."

I stood, needing to change clothes and figure out how I'm going to spend my day. It's only been four days since I was put on leave, and I feel lost. All I've ever known has been work. Now that I'm not going to the station, I'm not sure what to do.

"Tyler." Mom opened the door, a smile growing on her face. "This is such a pleasant surprise."

"I wanted to talk to you about something." I accepted her hug.

She locked the door and then ventured to the kitchen. "I talked to Harold about your leave from the force."

"Mom, I told you not to."

She held up her hand. "I wanted to know why he didn't stop it from happening."

"And?" I asked, curious myself.

"He said you were doing something reckless that he couldn't condone." She grinned mischievously. "And bringing Roxanne home will be easier without a badge holding you back."

I sat down heavily at the kitchenette. *Well, I'll be damned.* That was potentially the last thing I'd imagined my dad would say. Mom made coffee for us using a single-cup coffee machine that dad bought her for Christmas a few years back. She picked up both mugs and sat next to me.

"So, tell me, what have you been doing to bring your sister home?"

"Nico and I have been trying to figure that out." I hunched over my coffee. "The security placed on and around Rox is tight. We're having difficulties coming up with a plan."

"How is Nico holding up?"

The question didn't surprise me. She had asked me, out of earshot of Dad, how Nico was shortly after Rox's kidnapping. Back then, I was taken back by surprise. She scowled at me and explained that she knew Rox and Nico were engaged. That piece of information had infuriated me because I didn't know. Eventually, I begrudgingly accepted the engagement. It helps that I've witnessed Nico in a different light as he worked against his father to find clues about Roxanne's whereabouts.

"Better than he was." I answered. "There seems to be new life in him now that we know where Rox is."

She nodded. "What about Lexi? How is she holding up after Roxanne's surprise trip to the salon?"

"She was rightfully shaken but seems okay now." I looked over at Mom. "Lexi is actually the reason I came over. I want your advice."

She sat up a little straighter. "Again?"

"Well, the advice you gave me the other day really helped."

"That's good." She patted my hand. "What advice do you need this time?"

"I want to take Lexi on a date, but I don't want it to be a boring dinner and movie. Do you have any suggestions?"

"A date? With Lexi?" She repeated, uncertain she heard me right.

"Yes. We're in a relationship."

"This is who you were talking about the other night?" Mom narrowed her eyes at me. "Did you two start the relationship over the loss of your sister, her best friend?"

"Mom! How could you think that of me?" I asked incredulously.

"I only want to ensure you're doing this for the right reason." She explained. "She's had a difficult past, and I'd hate for it to be my son that breaks her."

"Mom." I took her hand and maintained eye contact. "I've been in love with Lexi since I first met her three years ago. Or maybe it was lust that turned into love. This was before I even knew she had a connection to my sister. Lexi walked away, but I never let go because I knew she was the one for me. Last night, she told me about her bad relationship in college, and it's only made me even more determined to make her happy."

Mom studied me, weighing my words in her head. "You're serious about her."

"I want to marry her." I smiled. "When she's ready to hear the question."

"There's a fair in Alexo this weekend." Mom smiled widely, squeezing my hand back. "I think Lexi will enjoy herself."

A fair. That's definitely not boring. I tossed the suggestion around in my head. I could picture her relaxed and having fun, and I could envision her smiling as I handed her a prize from a shooting game. *That will work.*

"Thanks, Mom." I stood kissing her cheek. "I got to go."

"Say hi to Lexi for me." She ordered with a laugh.

I rolled my eyes after I'd turned away. Somehow, after telling Mom about me and Lexi, I felt lighter. It was almost as if I was finally able to tell someone a secret that couldn't be kept silent any longer. I drove to Dagger Designs only to be told by Rita that Lexi was working at the other location this week. To be on the safe side, I called Lexi.

"Hi." She answered wistfully.

"Hi." I responded with a smile. "I want to take you out for lunch."

"Sorry, I already placed an order, and it's on its way over."

"Then I'll pick something up and come eat with you."

Lexi hesitated a millisecond. "How about dinner?"

Roxanne must be there. *I hate this.* I wish she would tell me about Rox instead of keeping it from me. Closing my eyes, I took a deep breath. *I have to trust her.*

"Sure. After work, come over to my place. I'll make you dinner." I said

"You can cook?"

"I'll surprise you with my skills, honey."

Lexi laughed. "I look forward to it."

I hung up with Lexi and drove to the grocery store. There was nothing in my fridge that I could use for a decent dinner. *What am I going to make?*

Fifteen

LEXI

I WOULD HAVE LOVED to have lunch with Tyler, but there's too much work to be done. As it is, Rossalyn and I will be having a working lunch. *Dinner. I can't wait.* I can't wait to see what Tyler cooks for me. No one has ever offered this before, so this will be a treat.

"Oh, I recognize that look." Rossalyn returned to the office with our ordered lunch.

"What look?"

"It's the look of a woman blissfully in love."

I frowned. "I'm not in love with anyone."

"Sure you're not." She rolled her eyes. "Then, whoever he is, he makes you very happy."

"He does." I admitted, a smile returning to my lips. "He's going to make me dinner tonight."

"Now that's a man worth keeping around."

I laughed.

"In all honesty, Lexi, you deserve something good in your life." Rossalyn said. "You've been so stressed with Roxanne disappearing and opening this salon. Happiness looks good on you."

"You've helped to relieve some stress." I told her, unwrapping the sub sandwich I'd ordered. "I don't think I would have been able to manage both Dagger Designs locations."

Rossalyn flushed. "Thank you for taking a chance on me."

Her previous job as a maid for one of the many wealthy families in Frostham didn't give her the experience I was looking for in a manager, but she applied for the job anyway. Rossalyn is cool-headed, organized, and a quick learner. This job may not pay as well as her previous one, but she's treated much better here — or so she claims.

"So, you were saying you wanted to make some changes to the staff?" I said, bringing our conversation back on track.

"Yes." Rossalyn lifted her power bowl from the desk to pull out some papers. "These two are not working out."

I looked at the papers. One was the employee sheet for the receptionist and the other for a nail tech. The receptionist shouldn't be too hard to replace, but the nail tech might be more of a challenge. *I'll have to contact Ethan.*

"Okay. What is the issue with Sarah and Jane?"

"Sarah is constantly on her phone, acts like she doesn't want to be here, and is always popping bubble gum while she talks." Rossalyn explained. "I've spoken to her multiple times about the phone and gum. I've even tried having her leave her phone in her locker, but she kept taking 'breaks' to go check it and wouldn't be at her post when a client called or walked in."

"Today is her last day." I said without hesitation. "I'll find a replacement immediately."

"My daughter can fill in while you look for a replacement."

I eyed Rossalyn. "This wasn't some ploy to find your daughter work, was it?"

"Of course not. You don't even have to pay her." Rossalyn protested. "She completed college as an administrative assistant and tried all summer to find a job. I thought this may be a good opportunity to give her some experience while she continues her search."

I knawed on my bottom lip, contemplating the offer. "Can your daughter start tomorrow?"

"Yes."

"I'll hire her on a temporary basis while I search for a permanent replacement." I shrugged. "Who knows, she may work out for a permanent position."

"Thank you, Lexi." Rossalyn smiled. "I will tell her tonight."

"Tell me about Jane."

"Jane is a sweet girl, but her clients have returned with complaints."

"What kind of complaints?"

"Nails are chipping or popping off a mere two days after their appointment." She frowned. "I've brought it up with Jane, but she doesn't know why."

"Dagger Designs has a reputation to uphold." I tossed out the wrapper from my lunch. "It's a good thing it has only been a soft opening."

"What should I do?"

"Nothing right now. I need to talk to Ethan Grekko at Clavus Schola. He's the director of the nail school and a friend of Roxanne's. He might know why the nails are popping off, and if he doesn't, then one of the teachers might. Either way, he might know someone I can hire as a replacement."

"I'm sorry I can't do better as a manager." Rossalyn said softly.

"You're doing just fine." I assured her. "Since this location has only been open for a couple of weeks, I expected a few bumps. Not these kinds of bumps, but better now than after the grand opening."

After work, I made my way to Tyler's. Nerves ate at my insides. Last night, Tyler announced he wanted more than sex. Sure, he's said before that he wanted a relationship with me, but I initially thought he referred to an exclusive bedmate. Similar to what Roxanne had with Jaylen.

Tyler Baxter wants a real relationship. With me. One that involves dates, emotions, and wooing. I couldn't wipe the smile from my face as I walked the steps up to his front door. *Tyler called me his woman.* I wiped sweaty palms on my jeans and knocked. I shouldn't be nervous, yet here I am, uncertain how Tyler and I will move forward.

Tyler answered the door with a frown. "You could have walked right on in."

"Well, uh." I felt my cheeks heat. "Things are different now."

"I disagree." He stepped aside. "Things are exactly as they should be."

"Oh."

"Lexi?"

"Yeah?"

Tyler cupped my face and kissed me. "I hope you're hungry."

My heart rate picked up. His kiss felt different, in a good way, as if he was more sure of himself. I couldn't stop the giddy smile that formed when he pulled away.

"You said you're cooking, right?"

A beeping sound pulled Tyler's attention. "The oven!"

I giggled as he rushed off. Lucky came scampering over, then plopped down to where Tyler last stood. I crouched down to scratch his head, then his belly, as he rolled onto his back.

"Let's go see what your owner is doing."

He barked, twisted up onto his paws and rushed off to the kitchen. I followed, stopping short. The counters were a mess with dirty dishes, pots on the stove bubbled away, and alarms were beeping. Tyler was busy turning off burners, alarms, and the overhead fan, all the while mumbling to himself. I took a seat at the table to watch the chaos unfold.

"Lexi!" Tyler called, turning with two plates in his hand. "Oh, sorry, I didn't realize you were there."

"You made quite a mess." I noted.

"I'm not much of a cook." A faint blush crept up his neck. "So I hope it's good."

"It's the thought that counts."

Tyler placed the plate in front of me. I leaned in, smelling the food appreciatively. Chicken parmesan with spaghetti. *How did he know this is my favourite?* Now, I have high expectations. Slicing into the chicken, I took my first bite.

When I opened my eyes — eyes I didn't realize had closed — Tyler was watching me. There was no expression on his face, no sign of playfulness in his eyes. His cop face stared back at me. I am really starting to hate that look. I miss the warmth that his eyes normally hold when he looks at me. As if realizing what he was doing, Tyler blinked, and everything shifted. Suddenly, his features softened, and his green eyes warmed. A shiver went down my spine at how eerie it was to watch the change.

"So?" He prompted. "How is it?"

"Satisfactory."

Tyler laughed. "The moan you admitted indicates it's more than satisfactory."

I felt my cheeks flame. "I moaned?"

A playful smirk curled his lips upward. "It nearly rivalled the moan you emit when I suck on your clit."

Need pooled low, causing me to shift in my seat. "There's no way that's accurate."

"A theory I'm more than willing to confirm." His eyes darkened at the suggestion.

"Nope." I stuck another piece of chicken in my mouth. "Not happening."

Tyler chuckled, slicing into his food. I couldn't help the grin that formed while watching his eyes widen. Clearly, he wasn't expecting the food to taste as good as it does. We ate and conversed about menial things. It felt comfortable and normal. *This is what real couples do, right?*

"I want to take you on a date." Tyler stated as he took my empty plate.

"A date?" I echoed.

"Nothing stiff or cliché like a dinner and a movie."

I got up to help him load the dishwasher. "Aren't we past the dating stage? I mean, we skipped right to the sex."

"My parents still go on dates. I remember when we were kids, Rox and I had a babysitter once a month." Tyler smiled, reminiscing on a good memory. "Rox would then dress up alongside mom. She would come bounding down the stairs, telling Dad that she was ready for her date. He would always tell her that that night was for him and Mom, but he promised Rox a different day would be for them."

"How much of a fuss did she make?"

"The usual little girl stuff of pouting and stomping her foot until that promise was made." Tyler grinned. "Now that I think about it. I think she might have had a small crush on our babysitter."

"What makes you say that?"

"All of her attention was turned onto the babysitter the moment he walked in."

I laughed. I was able to picture a tiny version of Roxanne perfectly, with her lip jutting out, arms crossed, and feet stomping. Then I could see her eyes widen in interest when the babysitter came in, and a smile would brighten her face. I'm sure it's the same look I remember seeing Rox wear when she talked about Nico before she lost her memory.

"What were you like as a child?" I asked.

Tyler rolled up his sleeves to begin washing the pots that were too big to fit the dishwasher. "I wasn't much of a troublemaker. Not with both my dad and grandfather working in the police force."

"Were they your inspiration to become a detective?" I grabbed a towel to dry what he had washed. "Or did you want to be something else?"

"I bounced around job options as most kids do. I wanted to be a fireman, a spy, or even a cowboy. For the longest time, I wanted to be a tattoo artist."

"Really? A tattoo artist?"

A smirk lifted his lips. "I'm sure you had a few odd dream jobs when you were a kid."

"I wanted to be a pageant queen or a model."

There was a heated look in his eyes when he took a leisurely look up and down my body. I felt the track of his eyes like a brand on my skin.

"I can see that." He said.

"So." I cleared my throat. "How did you become a detective?"

"I always had a mind for it. Rox and I both did." He explained. "We used to sneak into Dad's home office and play detective with the cases he brought home. The thing is, our playing actually helped to solve the cases because we saw something that was missed."

"I didn't know that."

"No one did." Tyler finished with the dishes, turned off the water, and gripped the sink, staring down at it. "That ended when our grandfather died. Dad changed. It wasn't until we were older that we learned the truth. I had decided that I'd be a detective so Dad would smile and praise me like he used to."

Tyler stopped, his heavy breaths shaking his body as he tried to control his emotions. I put the towel I was using down and stepped closer. I hesitated only a moment before wrapping my arms around him and resting my head on his back. Tyler placed a hand over mine, his muscles relaxing at my touch.

At that moment, as my heart softened at seeing his vulnerability and strength while he told me this story, I knew I'd never be able to walk away. The truth exploded in my head. *I love him.* It wasn't lust, longing, or the desire to find 'the one' that had me thinking about it. Maybe it was a combination of all of it that morphed into one base emotion — love.

"After learning the truth." Tyler continued. "My reasoning for becoming a detective changed."

"Oh?" I asked softly. "Why is that?"

"I wanted to help my dad catch my grandfather's murderer."

"Have you?"

"No, and we might never catch him."

"Why not?"

"It's Enzo Frangione, Nico's father." Tyler pulled me around to his front. "I'm sorry, Lexi, this conversation took a dark turn."

I shook my head, pushing up on tip-toe to kiss him. "Thank you for trusting me with your story."

Sixteen

TYLER

BLINDLY, I REACHED OVER to pull Lexi into me. Except, she wasn't there, and the space felt cold. Frowning, I opened my eyes. The bed was indeed empty, and the bathroom door was open. *Where is she?* I lay there listening for any sound of her in my house. Lucky barked on the other side of the bedroom door. *I should take him for a walk.* I kicked off the sheets about to respond to my dog when another voice did that for me.

"Shh." Lexi admonished. "You'll wake your owner."

Relief at the sound of her voice was almost embarrassing. I listened as her soft footfalls and Lucky's nails moved from the bedroom door and down the stairs. After last night I felt a shift in Lexi, though I wasn't sure what to make of it. Before, I felt like she was always ready to bolt, and after hearing what her ex did to her in college, I could understand why. Now, I'm not sure what she's going to do. I want to believe that we're even closer now that I've shared a piece of my past with her.

Only one way to find out. I slipped on a pair of sweatpants and ventured down to the kitchen. Lexi knelt on the floor, filling Lucky's bowl with his dry food. She petted his head and stood. Our eyes locked, and yet again, I felt a sense of rightness. If Lexi decides to run, I will follow and haul her back. Over my shoulder if I have to, and handcuff her to my bed until she understands that she belongs to me.

"Morning Tyler." She smiled sweetly at me.

That smile lit my world. That smile didn't reveal any doubt or fear. Maybe I'm the self-conscious one about her leaving me.

"Morning Lexi."

"I've already taken Lucky for a walk."

"Thanks." I pulled her into my arms for a kiss. "Now, about that date I mentioned last night."

"What were you thinking?" She wrapped her arms around my neck.

Her immediate acceptance surprised me, but I didn't let it show. I relaxed my shoulders. Clearly, I thought she was going to fight me on this. It has to be a good sign.

"There's a fair in Alexo this weekend." I said. "We can leave Friday when you're done work, maybe spend the night at a hotel, then come back Saturday."

"I'm helping Barbara with her wedding on Saturday. She has a final dress fitting that her sister can't make. Then she wants help with the seating chart."

"What time do you need to meet up with her?"

Lexi pulled from my arms so she could check her phone. "The dress fitting is at eleven."

"I'll make sure you're back in Frostham in time."

She smiled again. "Thanks, Tyler."

I frowned. "You know, you've never once called me Ty."

"No, I haven't." She confirmed.

"Why is that?"

"Your sister and your best friend shorten your name. I never had the right to do so."

"As my woman." I pulled her back into my arms. "You have the right to call me whatever you want."

"How about calling you my man?" She wrapped her arms around my neck again.

"I like the sound of it."

I kissed her hard, overwhelmed with possessiveness and love for this woman. Lexi accepted everything I gave her and returned it with the same amount of zeal. Lucky barked, and I felt his paw on my knee. Breaking apart, I looked down at my dog. He stood on his hind legs, front paws on both Lexi and me, while his tail wagged happily. Lexi laughed, reaching down to pet his head.

"I need to get to work, Ty."

I grinned, loving my name on her lips. "Say it again."

Lexi smiled indulgently. "I will see you Friday, Ty."

"Wait, why Friday?" I questioned.

"For our date." She said, collecting her purse. "Have you forgotten already?"

"That's still two days away."

"Your point?"

I followed her to the front door. "I want you in my bed every night."

"Friday." Lexi said again, cupping my cheek and giving me a chaste kiss. "If I'm always with you, then my apartment gets neglected."

She left before I could blurt out the words that were on the tip of my tongue. If she moved in with me, then she wouldn't have to worry about her apartment. I wasn't sure how she'd take the offer. She may accept it with a smile, or it could make her cautious again.

I looked down at Lucky. "Well, bud, it's just you and me for the next couple of days."

Nico invited me out for lunch. He's only ever reached out if he had information on Roxanne. So this had to be about Rox. *Why here?* I entered the gastro pub, looking around and finding him already seated in a booth. The restaurant was loud. Whatever he had to say would be drowned out by the noise. Next to him sat a brunette who looked far too high maintenance for his place.

"Tyler, this is my sister Candi." Nico introduced us immediately. "She said she had something important to tell us."

For a millisecond, I thought Nico was cheating on my sister. After that quick introduction, I knew it was a stupid thought. Upon closer inspection, the siblings have the same eyes. Besides, Nico would never cheat on Roxanne. I've seen the love he has for her. I'd be stupid to ignore it. He'd be even stupider to cheat on Rox.

"Nice to meet you, Candi." I slid into the booth opposite them.

A waitress came by and placed two hamburgers and a wrap on the table. I looked at the food, then at Nico.

"I went ahead and ordered." He explained. "This way, we won't be interrupted quite so often."

I nodded. "I take it this is extremely important."

"It's about Roxanne."

I turned my gaze to his sister. "You know Roxanne?"

"I do." She said, stabbing at her side salad. "She became my nail technician after a nail catastrophe at another salon."

"Tell us what you know." Nico prompted. "All of it."

Candi began eating. Nico and I stared expectantly at her. With an annoyed-sounding sigh, she put her wrap down.

"The other day, I had my nail appointment at Dagger Designs." Candi said. "To my surprise, Roxanne was there. Something felt off about her. Before she left the salon with Lexi, Lexi whispered in my ear to visit Franco."

I was, figuratively, on the edge of my seat. "Well? Did you visit Franco?"

"I did."

"And?" I pushed. "What did you find out?"

Candi pursed her lips, appearing not to want to continue. She looked to Nico, who only raised a single brow. The two of them stared at each other in silent communication.

"Fine." Candi huffed. "I got around to visiting Franco yesterday. I should have known better than to stop by unannounced when he has a woman."

Candi visibly shivered at the memory. I had a suspicion she meant that she walked in on Franco and Roxanne in a compromising position. Based on Nico's dark scowl, he was thinking the same thing. It shouldn't be unexpected. If Franco wanted to maintain the illusion of marriage, sex would be involved. The thought of it makes my skin crawl. Hearing about it only makes it worse.

"Anyway." Candi continued. "I learnt about Roxanne's memory loss and their supposed marriage. I couldn't believe it, not when I'd seen her with Nico a few months ago at the Cantoni birthday, but there was no way I could question Roxanne with Franco right there."

I slumped in my seat. "I don't see how we're going to free my sister from Franco's clutches."

"I don't know if this will help." Candi picked up her wrap nonchalantly. "Franco agreed that next weekend I can take Roxanne away on a bachelorette-style girl's get-away. As long as he knows where I'm taking her and Andrew is with us the entire time."

I stared at Candi awestruck, then turned to Nico, who also stared at his sister. *This is it.* Nico and I can make a solid plan to kidnap Rox and jog her memory. With Candi's help, we'll know exactly where she will be and when.

"What?" Candi asked, looking between us.

"You need to tell us your schedule for that weekend." Nico instructed. "We are going to free Roxanne from Franco and bring her back to where she belongs."

Seventeen

LEXI

TODAY WAS A GOOD day. It was Friday, Roxanne was working beside me, and tonight, Tyler was taking me on a date. I was hesitant because my past dates were either boring or very bad. But this is Tyler, and he's taking me to a fair. I've never been to a fair before. It should be fun.

"You seem to be in a chipper mood." Roxanne noted as we filled out inventory sheets.

"I have a date tonight." I announced proudly.

She frowned. "Another potential bad date from a dating app?"

"No, I deleted those. This is someone I met in real life."

"Is it with Andrew?" She elbowed me playfully. "Did he finally wear you down? I saw him kiss you the other night."

"Absolutely not." I scowled at her. "This date is with some-one I feel a real connection with."

"Well, spill, who is it?"

I shook my head. "I've never told you the names of my past dates. Why would I start now?"

"Fine." Rox huffed. "At least tell me where he is taking you?"

"There's a fair in Alexo."

"Oh! Speaking of Alexo." Roxanne snapped her fingers. "Candi is taking me there next weekend for a bachelorette thing. Since I didn't have one before my marriage."

I stopped inventory to stare at her. "Franco is allowing you out of the city?"

"I will be with you ladies the entire time." Andrew an-nounced behind us. "Here are your coffees."

"Andrew." Rox scolded. "You ruined it."

"My apologies, Mrs. Frangione."

"Ruined what?" I asked while accepting the coffee.

"Candi is inviting Brina, and I want you to join us too." Rox said. "It'll be so much fun having a girls' weekend."

It took my brain a minute to register the words, but when they did, I couldn't believe the opportunity. I could spend a whole weekend with Roxanne to work on restoring her memory. *I'm not passing on this opportunity.*

"Yes." I said. "I'd love to join you."

"I will be chauffeuring you ladies to Alexo." Andrew said. "Miss Candi is still finalizing a few details. I will need to pick you up next Friday at noon."

I nodded and turned to Rox. "I'll need to know Candi's plans so I can pack accordingly."

"I'll see what I can find out." She promised.

"So, Lexi." Andrew hedged. "Do you have any plans for tonight? I'll be off duty at six. We could go out for dinner."

"I have plans." I said.

"She has a date." Roxanne divulged. "I guess you missed your chance, Andrew. That kiss you planted on her didn't have much of an effect. Or, maybe you should have taken my offer to help win Lexi over."

"I haven't lost yet." Andrew stated confidently. "The date can still turn sour."

"True."

"Hey, I'm right here." I complained.

"She's been humming while we work." Rox said. "I think you're too late."

"We'll see." Andrew winked at me before walking away to sit somewhere out of the way.

"You have to give him points for the confidence."

"And deduct points for the lack of interest on my side." I said.

"Really? Nothing about him turns you on?" She hedged. "That kiss did nothing for you? It looked pretty steamy from my view."

"He's good-looking." I agreed, glancing over at him. "But I don't think he's got the stuff I'm looking for in a man."

"You never know unless you give him a chance."

"It's not in the cards."

Roxanne let out a puff of breath. "You've gone on plenty of dates looking for 'the one', and no one has measured up. Maybe you should try a different approach."

I frowned at her, not liking that she was pushing Andrew on me. "And what do you suggest?"

"Start with sex. If there's no connection there, then he's definitely not the man for you."

I resisted the urge to laugh. That's how it worked with Tyler. When he took me to bed, I was hooked. No one could compare to him. I only looked around for someone else because he was Rox's brother, but I could never forget him. I took another covert look over at Andrew. Would the same thing happen if I took Andrew to bed? My initial thought of him was that I'd flirt back if Tyler wasn't in the picture. I shook my head. *This is ridiculous.* I need to squash Andrew's flirtatious nature and fast. I have Tyler. There's no one else I need or want aside from him.

Tyler was at my door at six o'clock, looking delicious in a green plaid button-down shirt with a green tie. It made his green eyes look even more green.

"Fancy." I teased, tugging his tie to lower him for a kiss.

He grinned into the kiss. "You look stunning."

Jeans and a blue top aren't worthy of the word stunning, but I'll take the compliment. I grabbed the small purse that I'd put the essentials into — like my ID, keys, and lipgloss — from the kitchen counter and was ready to go. After locking up, Tyler laced his fingers in mine and led me to his car.

Alexo is a little over an hour away from Frostham. For the entire drive, Tyler kept his fingers linked with mine. Letting go when he needed two hands on the steering wheel. He showed off his evasive driving skills to avoid a pickup truck that didn't believe in side mirrors. We made it to the fair in one piece.

"So." Tyler flung his arm over my shoulder after buying tickets at the front gate. "Do you want to start with some food? Then we can wander the fair to scope out the games."

"As long as we hit the Ferris wheel." I smiled up at him. "I've always wanted to go on one."

"I wouldn't dare deny you the opportunity."

There were so many sounds, smells, and lights at the fair. It was overwhelming and exciting all at once. Because I had never been to a fair before, I didn't know where to begin, so I let Tyler take the lead. We passed by various game booths to the center of the fair, where food trucks were set up to feed the crowd.

"What are you in the mood for?" Tyler asked.

"I have no idea." I admitted. "What's the most fair-like food?"

"Anything deep fried."

I laughed. Someone walked by with a plate of what looked like spiralled potatoes. I looked back up at Tyler to ask him about it when he ordered me to sit down and wait. He plopped me down on one of many picnic benches for fair goes to eat at, then went to buy us food.

While I waited, one guy sat down across from me and tried to flirt, but when Tyler arrived, he paled and skittered off. I couldn't help but laugh. Tyler took his spot, placed a plate of spiralled potatoes on the table, and handed me something on a stick.

"What is this?" I eyed the item.

"It's called a corn dog, and it tastes best with mustard." Tyler handed me a mustard pack. "Have you never heard of a corn dog?"

"Heard of them. Never seen or eaten one before."

"You're in for a treat. This is quintessential fair food."

I squeezed the mustard along the length of the corn dog and took my first bite. *It's different.* I examined the inside. A hot dog dipped in a batter and then deep-fried. It's not horrible, but it wouldn't be my first choice of food. It also didn't stop me from eating the whole thing. *I can say I've had one now.* The potatoes were much tastier.

"Let's go play some games." Tyler said when we finished eating. "Our stomachs can settle before we ride some rides."

"Works for me."

There were so many games to choose from. Fishing games, ring toss games, shooting games, and balloon pop games. No two booths were the same. The shooting games are where Tyler shined. His years as a cop, wielding a gun and training with it, helped him to win prizes. At most booths, I gave the award he or I had won to the little kid who couldn't succeed. What was I to do with all the stuffies? My arms weren't big enough.

"That teddy bear is massive." I pointed to a three-foot-tall bear with a big red bow. "He's probably hard to win."

Tyler tugged me over to the game booth with the bear. "What does one have to do to win the giant teddy bear?"

The person in charge of the booth grinned. "See the five tiny moving targets? Hit each one, and you win the bear."

"Sounds easy enough."

"After the third target goes down, the speed of the targets goes up."

"Tyler, you don't have to win the bear." I said, doubtful that he'd win.

He grinned at me. "Think of me when you hug him at night."

My cheeks heated. Tyler handed over the necessary tickets and was given five corks to use as bullets in the modified gun for the game. His expression morphed into one of concentration as he lined up the first shot. Bullseye. Same with targets two and three. When the targets moved faster, I wasn't sure he'd hit the target. I was wrong.

Down goes target four. *Only one more.* I wanted to grip his arm and shake him with the excitement I was feeling. He was so close. But I refrained from breaking his concentration. Barely. The targets began moving even faster. *That's impossibly fast.* Tyler took a deep, slow breath, eyes focused on the target.

"You did it." I said, not believing it at first. "You did it!"

Tyler put the modified gun down, turning to me with a shit-eating grin. I jumped on him, wrapping my arms around his neck and kissed him. Tyler caught me effortlessly and kissed me back.

The booth person cleared his throat. "That was impressive."

"Thanks." Tyler said, putting me down and accepting the giant teddy bear. "Here you are, Lexi."

I hugged the bear in my arms. "Thanks, Ty."

"Anything to see you smile." Tyler pecked my lips. "Now, let's go fit in a few rides before we head out."

He guided me toward the back of the fair, where all of the rides were set up. There was a carousel, a swing-style ride, a tea cup-style ride, something called a zipper, and a handful of other fun-looking rides. Of course, the ride I want to ride the most is the Ferris wheel. *Where should we begin?*

The staff manning the rides were kind enough to watch over the teddy bear Tyler had won for me while we rode the ride they were in charge of. I was having so much fun. The wind blew my hair around my face as the ride spun its riders around and up in the air.

Finally. I stared up at the Ferris wheel while Tyler and I waited in line. With the teddy bear in my arms and Tyler's arm around my waist, I was hopping on the balls of my feet. I couldn't wait. The line moved in groups of two to four. Finally, at the front, Tyler and I entered the enclosed box.

"Excited?" Tyler asked as the wheel began to move.

"Very." I kept my eyes on the window.

The wheel moved slowly as it let on its riders. When it stopped at the top, I sat a little closer to the edge. *Stunning.* The lights of Alexo sparkled in the night like little diamonds, a reflection of the stars in the sky.

"This has been really fun, Tyler." I tore my eyes from the window to see him staring at me. "What?"

"You take my breath away." He said.

Eighteen

TYLER

I DROPPED LEXI off at her apartment with plenty of time to get ready before going out to meet Barbara. After last night, I was on cloud nine. The date went even better than I'd have dreamed. It'll be a challenge to top that date.

I went home to change clothes. With Lucky at my parents' house, my place was eerily quiet. *I should have invited Lexi to move in with me last night.* With Lexi brightening it up, my home would feel even more like home. I smiled at the idea.

"Hey, Mom." I called, entering the house. "I'm here for Lucky."

"We're in the living room." She called back.

I walked into the living room. Mom was on the couch, her legs pulled up, and she held an open book in one hand while the other petted Lucky. The beagle was tucked in the crook of her knees, his head on her lap. It was a picturesque scene — a scene I had seen before with Lexi. It was the night I caught her scrolling through a dating app. That reminds me, I haven't checked to make sure she deleted that useless app.

"How was your date with Lexi?"

I felt a goofy grin spread across my face. "Your suggestion of the fair was brilliant."

"I'm glad."

"Watching her experience the fair and try a corn dog for the first time." I took a seat in an armchair. "It was fun."

She smiled. "I'm happy for you."

"Thanks, Mom."

We chatted for a while before my phone rang. "Baxter."

"Nico's been arrested." Jaylen whispered.

"What? Why?"

Jaylen hung up without answering. *What the hell?* I tried calling my partner back but couldn't get through.

"What's wrong?" Mom asked.

"I'm not sure." I admitted, getting up and kissing her cheek. "Can you keep Lucky for a little while longer? I'm going to head to the station and find out what's going on."

"Sure. I hope everything is okay."

"Me too." I petted Lucky. "I'll see you later bud."

Lucky lifted his head, tilting it back to lick my hand. I left Mom and went to the station. When I arrived, the tension in the air was thick. Officers spoke in hushed tones while in groups of two or three. Something big must have happened because all this couldn't be due to Nico.

"Jaylen." I tapped a knuckle on his desk. "What's going on?"

He looked around carefully before looking at me. "Enzo Frangione is here."

"He's what?" Disbelief was evident in my outburst. "Why?"

"Probably to free his son from assault charges." Jaylen shrugged. "He's in the Captain's office."

I looked toward Dad's office. It was tempting to storm into that office and demand that he order Franco to give us back Roxanne. Except, I doubt that'll work. It'll also interfere with the plan Nico and I are cooking up.

"Where are you going?" Jaylen called after me.

"To the holding cells."

Jaylen followed, an official shadow, since without my badge, I technically don't have the right to roam the station. Nico sat on the edge of the cot in the cell, elbows on his knees, his leg shaking. He looked up when I stopped at his cell door.

"You're not supposed to be in here." I accused, crossing my arms.

"Accommodations could be better." He countered, standing to meet me at the bars. "You wouldn't happen to be here to offer me an upgrade?"

I took better stock of his dishevelled appearance. There was blood on his dress shirt and a cut on his lip, and his knuckles looked well-used.

"How bad is the other guy?"

Nico scowled. "Still alive."

"Police arrived at Obsidian to find him in a brawl." Jaylen stated. "They had to force him off the guy. In the process, he hit the officers."

"It was an accident." Nico snarled.

"Now you're behind bars where you belong."

"Except Enzo is here." I cut in.

Nico looked like he'd been slapped across the face with that piece of news. "I can't leave here with him. I don't even want to imagine what he'll do to me for the trouble I've caused."

I blinked only to verify that it was fear I saw in Nico's eyes. *Yep, that's fear.* There's only one way to free the man from this cell without handing him over to his father, and it's not strictly legal. In fact, I could wind up in jail next to Nico if I'm not quick. I was contemplating how to get rid of Jaylen when an officer came to fetch him.

"Okay, Ty, your time here is up." He said.

"One more minute. There's still something I need to say to Nico."

Jaylen narrowed his eyes. "Make it quick. I don't want to see you here when I return."

"You won't." I promised.

I waved him off and watched him leave. When he was out of sight, I pulled out my car keys and used the bump key attached to them. I wiggled the key into the lock, then carefully turned it. Using my palm, I bumped the end until the key could turn properly. At the click, I grinned and removed the key.

"So, that's where Roxanne learnt it." Nico mused under his breath.

"No time to chat." I pulled the door open and yanked Nico out of the cell. "We don't have much time to get out of here."

"Tyler." He started to protest but followed anyway.

"Shut up. I'm saving my sister's fiancée, who in turn will save her."

"Thank you." Nico whispered.

The back doors to the holding cells are used to get high-profile criminals out of the station. Captain Baxter holds press conferences to keep journalists occupied and away from the back alley. So far, no journalist has figured out the diversionary tactic.

Jaylen's loud string of prolific curses reached my ears just as the back door was closing. *It won't be long now.* Nico and I practically ran down the short hall, then flew down the stairs to the back alley. My car was parked a block away instead of in visitor parking, which is quite telling in this situation. Something I don't care to examine.

Nico and I had to lay low until the weekend. That's when we'll rescue Roxanne. This act of rebellion on my part can be looked over once she's back. If we fail, Dad won't be able to help me when I'm arrested alongside Nico.

"Head to Royal Heights." Nico ordered.

"Why?"

"We can hide your car in my cousin's garage and borrow one of theirs to get to Alexo."

I shook my head. "Unless your cousin is willing to go to jail for aiding and abiding, I suggest another tactic."

"What do you suggest, then?"

"The airport. We can leave my car in long-term parking and then catch a cab back into the city. Are you able to provide a new vehicle?"

"I'll need to make a phone call." Nico held out his hand. "My stuff is still at the station."

I pulled out my phone from my pocket and handed it to him. He spoke to someone in Italian before handing it back to me. At the airport, I texted Lexi.

> **Me:** I'm sorry for what I'm about to do. I'll explain later. Please trust me.

> **Me:** Also, can you watch over Lucky? He's with Mom.

> **Me:** I promise that in one week, everything will be back to normal, and I'll make it up to you.

I couldn't wait for a reply. I pulled the battery out of my phone. As of this moment, Nico and I have gone dark.

Nineteen

LEXI

THE WEEK flew BY. I was so busy with Dagger Designs that I didn't have time to miss Tyler during the day. At night, I missed having his body next to mine. After receiving his cryptic texts last week, I tried reaching out to him, but his phone was out of service. The radio silence made me self-conscious. *He's doing it again.* I fear that he didn't feel like our date at the fair was as emotionally profound as I felt it was.

Lucky barked up at me, pulling me from my darkening thoughts. With a faint smile, I bent down to scratch his head. Tyler wouldn't abandon Lucky. With the dog entrusted to me, I know I'll see the owner again. I made arrangements with Jenna to check in on the beagle while I spent the weekend with Roxanne, Candi and Brina. I feel sorry for the dog. Lucky has been moved between Tyler's home, his parent's place, and my place too often lately. There hasn't been any consistency for him.

I zipped up my small bag containing two days' worth of clothes and placed it by the front door seconds before there was a knock. Lucky came running up behind me. He sniffed at the bottom crack of the door, let out a growl, and began barking consistently. It was almost as if he was warning me of danger on the other side of the door.

"It's okay, Lucky." I used my foot to push him away from the door.

Andrew stood on the other side, smiling down at me. "Are you ready to go, Lexi?"

"Yes, let me grab my bag."

I opened the door wider, turning to grab my bag. Lucky continued to bark, rushing past me to stand at the threshold. He really doesn't like Andrew. Not that I blame him. I don't like him much either. Andrew looked down at Lucky, then back to me with a raised brow.

"Lucky!" I scolded, sweeping the dog up in my arms. "I'm sorry, Andrew."

"I didn't know you had a dog."

"Only as of recently."

I managed to push my bag toward him with my foot. Andrew bent to pick up the bag, and his nearness caused Lucky to growl his disapproval. I returned to the kitchen to grab the small purse I'd prepared. Back at the door, I put Lucky down with a gentle toss to give me enough time to close the door before he came running back to it.

"Will he be okay?" Andrew asked as Lucky continued to bark.

"He just doesn't like you." I locked the door and then turned to him.

"That's too bad. I like dogs."

Ignoring that comment, I answered his question. "I have someone coming to check on him while I'm away this weekend."

"What made you decide to get a dog?"

"I fell in love at first sight." I pushed the elevator button and changed the subject. "Is Roxanne waiting in the car?"

"Mr. Frangione ordered me to pick you up first so he can spend a little more time with his wife."

I inwardly cringed. The elevator opened, and we stepped in. The longer Roxanne is in Franco's clutches, the harder it may become to awaken her memories. I'm afraid she'll get Stockholm syndrome if she's with him much longer. This weekend is crucial. I really hope Candi will help me.

"What has you so deep in thought?" Andrew's voice pierced through my musings.

"Huh?" I blinked up at him. "Oh. Nothing important."

He grinned down at me, that dimple showing, and his brown eyes darkened. "Then you should fill that pretty head of yours with thoughts of me instead."

"I'd rather not. You're not that important."

"I could be."

The elevator door opened to the lobby, and I couldn't get out fast enough. The downside to my apartment building is that all of its parking is outside, including the reserved spots for the residents.

"Where did you park your car?"

"This way." He jerked his head to the left. "Visitor parking."

I followed behind him. *Note to self: don't get caught alone with Andrew.* Something tells me that he'll take any opportunity to try and win me over. Words he used the first time we met. This weekend will be the best opportunity for him because I won't have anywhere to run.

Andrew stopped at a limousine. I nearly tripped over my feet at the sight of it. I've never been inside a limo. Andrew held the back door open for me, and I slid inside. *Rich people.* I ran my hand over the smooth, butter-soft leather seats. I'm really not impressed with these luxuries, but I appreciate them on these rare occasions. I heard the front door close and then felt the subtle rumble of the engine coming to life.

A privacy screen rolled down. "Lexi."

"Yes?" I looked up to catch Andrew's eyes in the rearview mirror.

"That date you had, was it good?"

"Very much so."

"Then there's room for improvement."

"Doubtful."

"Well, if he's not satisfying you, I'd be more than willing to take over that honour."

I scowled at him. "No thanks, I'm good."

There was a sparkle of challenge in his eyes. "You'll come around."

"Don't waste your efforts on me, Andrew."

"Time with you is never a waste."

"You need to stop. I'm never going to fall into bed with you." I tried to deter him from any further flirting.

"Never say never."

I glared and crossed my arms. *He just won't give up.* Andrew winked, then rolled up the privacy screen before driving away. This is going to be a very long weekend. I won't be able to let my guard down around him.

Candi had our entire evening planned. After having our bags delivered to the hotel, we did some shopping — including clothes for a club later in the evening — our purchases were immediately sent to the hotel. Then, it was a trip to a spa to be pampered from head to toe, and then it was dinner at a highly recommended restaurant by her followers.

I surprised myself by how much fun I was having. Candi is actually a decent person when she drops her influencer persona. Rox, Candi, and I got changed for the club in the back of the limo. Brina was to meet us at the club. She would have joined us during the day but already had plans that she couldn't back out of.

"You ladies look beautiful." Andrew complemented as he helped each of us out of the limo.

"Of course." Candi responded, flipping her brown hair over her shoulder. "Nothing less would be expected."

Rox and I rolled our eyes. Candi's haughty influencer personality was shining through. Andrew smiled indulgingly. Candi looped an arm with Roxanne and led the way to the club, telling us that Brina was waiting inside. Andrew walked slightly behind us. I could feel Andrew's eyes on me the entire walk from the limo to the club, which was only a couple of blocks away. It made me wish I'd picked a longer dress, but I was thinking of Tyler when I bought it. The line for the club curled around the building, yet instead of waiting in that long line, Candi was taking us straight to the front.

"Alexis?"

An icy chill ran up my spine at that voice, freezing me in place. I haven't heard that voice or that name since college. *I'm hallucinating.* Needing to confirm that I was hearing things, I slowly turned to the line of people. A man with a square jaw, brown eyes and a pudgy figure stared at me expectantly. He had his arm slung over some blonde woman with red lips and breasts too large for her slim figure. I couldn't breathe. It may have been years since I saw him, but I will always recognize Bradley. My ex from college.

"It is you." He smiled triumphantly while his eyes greedily took in my body. "You're looking fantastic."

"Do you know him?" Andrew asked.

I jumped, startled out of my panic. "He's an ex."

Andrew simply nodded. Placing a hand on my lower back, he gently urged me forward. Candi and Rox were already at the front of the line. Rox was watching me with a frown. I tried to clear my expression and smile. There's no need for her to be concerned. It didn't work. Her frown only deepened. *I could really use Tyler right now.* Thinking of him put a little courage in my step. *I am Tyler's woman.* Bradley doesn't deserve a second of my time.

"Hey, buddy." Bradley called after us. "I could give you some bedroom tips for that one."

"Not needed." Andrew responded.

"She's a dud root if you don't heat her up just right."

"Lexi, go inside the club." He growled.

As crude and embarrassing as Bradley's comment was, he doesn't deserve the wrath of an ex-black-ops. Besides, if I let

Andrew defend me, he might use it against me. I don't want to owe him anything. Not even a debt of gratitude.

"Ignore him." I said, the words forced out of my throat. "He doesn't deserve any attention."

"He insulted you."

"He's my ex for a reason."

"Fine." Andrew grumbled.

The moment I was within reach, Rox took my hand and pulled me into the club with Candi. Brina was waiting for us in a private area. Shots were immediately ordered. They were a pleasant burn down my throat. With the alcohol, thrumming music, and company, I was able to relax again.

The best part of any club is the dancing. Rox and I danced until our feet blistered. And the alcohol flowed like water among our group. All four of us were pretty drunk by the time Andrew declared it was time to go and hurdled us back to the limo.

I leaned heavily into Andrew as he corralled us to our hotel room. The alcohol had my vision blurring and my steps uneasy. He kept an arm around me to keep me upright.

"Now, if you ladies need anything." Andrew said as he opened our hotel room. "My room is just across the hall."

"Okay." Brina giggled.

When the door shut, I swear Brina and Candi sobered instantly. Or maybe they weren't really drunk. Then, why fake it? They were busy stuffing today's purchases into our respectful bags.

"What are you doing?" Rox asked before falling face-first onto a bed.

"I want to take you somewhere special." Candi said, rolling her over. "But first, we need to send Andrew away."

"He is away, silly."

"Further away."

Brina was eyeing me like I was the newest fashion trend. "Lexi can do it."

"Nope." I shook my head emphatically, then groaned at the headache it caused. "I'm not going anywhere near him."

"The way he was watching you at the club, he'll probably do anything you ask."

"Yep." Rox agreed, sitting up. "Andrew really wants Lexi."

"Perfect." Candi said. "Getting him out of the hotel is your job."

"What? Why?" I argued. "How am I supposed to do that?"

"I don't know. Tell him you want French Fries to help alleviate the hangover. He must walk out of this hotel soon."

"French Fries." I mumbled.

Before I knew it, Brina had pushed me out of the door with a keycard to our room stuffed into my hand. I stood there a minute contemplating re-entering the room. *There has to be a reason.* I don't know what Candi has planned, but whatever it is, it seems pretty urgent because of the way she rushed to pack our bags. So, I took the few steps necessary to cross the hall and knocked on Andrew's door. He opened it, and all I could do was stare at his bare chest. Muscled and hair-free and broad. It was a glorious sight to behold.

"Lexi, now this is a surprise." He said, amusement in his tone.

"French Fries." I blurted.

"Excuse me?"

I reached out, running my fingers along the ridges of his muscles. It was fascinating how they tensed under my gentle touch. Andrew sucked in a sharp breath. I licked my lips, trailing my fingers down his abs. The alcohol was really impeding my common sense because there was no way I would have done this sober. *Think of Tyler, you're his woman.* Some food should help to sober me up.

"French Fries." I repeated.

"Is that your safe word?"

"Too much of a mouthful." I looked up at him. "I want you to get me French Fries."

Voices could be heard down the hall. Andrew wrapped a hand around my wrist and tugged me into his room, then closed the door behind me. My heart rate picked up. I was officially alone with him. This is the exact situation I wanted to avoid, yet I stepped right into it.

We stood there, looking at each other. He still held my wrist, which was still touching his abs. *What am I doing?* Andrew is only inches away. I pulled away and moved further into his hotel room. I was beginning to feel claustrophobic standing there in such an enclosed spot with him standing so close.

"Lexi, you're drunk." He said, following me.

"I'm sober enough to know what I want." I lied.

"Hmm, are you now?" Andrew mused, running his hands up my arms and kissing my shoulder.

"Yes." I agreed, shivering at his touch. "And I want French Fries."

"I'll have to leave the hotel to fetch you your French Fries. That will leave all of you ladies unprotected."

"Sacrifices must be made for the sake of fries."

Andrew spun me around. His brown eyes searched my face for some unknown answer to the unspoken question in his head. I hoped my eyes didn't reveal how uncomfortable I am right now.

"How badly do you want those fries?" He questioned.

I pouted. "Will you not get them for me?"

"One kiss for every fry." He countered, brushing his thumb over my bottom lip.

My stomach clenched. I don't want to kiss him, but Candi wants him gone. There has to be a reason. Every move I have made since knocking on his door has been giving him the wrong signals. There's still an opening for me to back away.

"I guess you don't want those fries that badly." Andrew said, taking a step back.

I panicked. I'm supposed to be getting Andrew out of the hotel. If kissing him is the only way to do it, then I'll take one for the team. I can always wash my mouth out with soap and mouthwash later. *This better be worth it, Candi.* I grabbed Andrew's head with both hands, pulling it down to mash my lips onto his. For extra measure, I pressed my chest into his. Andrew reacted instantly. He slid his hand up my thighs and under my dress to grip my ass. He lifted me off the ground, spun and pressed me into the wall, all while kissing me back. The intensity of his kiss had me reeling.

"This isn't what I meant." He said, his lips trailing down my neck.

"I want those French Fries." I replied, trying to stay focused.

"I wanted to kiss every inch of your skin. One kiss per fry."

I tucked a hand under his jaw, forcing his head back up. "You should have said that sooner."

He fused our mouths back together. It was impossible to breathe. All the air in my lungs was stolen by this kiss with Andrew. I opened my mouth, hoping to suck in some much-needed air, and he took full advantage to deepen the kiss. Andrew wrapped my legs around his waist, then slid his hands back up my legs. His thumbs caressed sensually along the edge of my panties. An unwanted whimper slipped out. *This is wrong.* My mind screamed at me. *I need to stop.* I tried to lower my feet to the ground, but Andrew wouldn't let me.

"I need you, Lexi." He said hoarsely.

He gripped my hips more tightly and pressed into me. I could feel Andrew's cock pressing against his jeans, straining to be freed. Hard and throbbing at my core. *I need to push him away.* This was getting far too heated, way too fast. I needed this to slow down. I needed this to stop.

"I need Franch Fries." I said, breathing heavily.

"I'll bring you back a small fry."

"Small fry?" I squeaked. "That kiss was worthy of a medium, at least."

I don't know why I argued. I was only supposed to get him out of the hotel, and I succeeded, yet I got greedy with my food. Andrew smiled, returning to my lips. He pulled me from the hard surface of the wall and placed me on the soft surface of his bed.

I lowered my arms and tried to squirm out from under him. *It's too much. This is going too far.* Andrew took my hands, gripping both wrists in one of his hands above my head. His free hand pressed down on my abdomen while he pressed his erection into me. *I don't want this.*

"I'll get you your fries." Andrew said. "All you have to do is stay here."

He pulled back, and I sat up on my knees, watching him pull on a shirt. *Leave already.* Andrew stopped by the bed, his brown eyes roaming over my body. Darkened with lust and a steely determination.

"One more for the road." He said before leaning in to kiss me again.

Andrew is an excellent kisser. I couldn't deny him that, but I shouldn't be wanting his kiss. I almost told him to forget the fries. I kept my hand clasped behind me as he brushed his lips against mine. I'm sure he intended the kiss to be quick. Andrew had me pressed back into the mattress, his hands spreading my legs as he settled in between them.

"I really don't want to leave." He admitted.

I swallowed back the whimper. It might be taken the wrong way. I should have never come over here. I need to get out of here. *I'm such an idiot.*

"But you earned those fries." He pressed another kiss to my lips. "I'll be right back."

I watched him leave. The door clicked shut, and I waited two breaths before rushing to the door. I had to grab the key card I had dropped at some point during my time in his room before I could exit. I regret the kiss and regret not arguing against Candi and Brina more. I will not stick around and wait for Andrew. I crashed back into the room I shared with the other women and made a beeline for the bathroom. I needed to wash the taste of Andrew off of me.

"Are you okay?" Candi asked, a hint of concern in her voice.

"That had better have been worth it." I scowled at her. "I nearly sold my body for French Fries."

There was a knock on the door, and Candi went to answer it.

Twenty

TYLER

NICO AND I STAYED under the radar in Alexo all week. He used connections I didn't know he had to keep us hidden. His connections got us a car and a motel in Alexo. They even supplied us with cash so we don't leave a paper trail. The hardest part for me was staying away and out of touch with Lexi. I wanted desperately to call her and hear her voice. I could have used a burner phone, but I didn't want to risk staying on for too long. I doubt she's on the cop's radar. No one knows about my relationship with her. It still killed me not being able to reach out. She probably hates me for ghosting her — again.

Nico used a burner phone to communicate with his sister, Candi, and other parties involved in the rescue of Roxanne. We will take my sister back on Friday at The Grand Hotel in Alexo. Nico had made connections in the city who would help keep Andrew away long enough for us to get in and get out. All Candi will have to do is send Andrew on some errand, forcing him to leave the women alone.

Finally, Friday came. Nico and I waited until late in the evening to drive from our motel to The Grand Hotel. We took up residence in the hotel bar, positioning ourselves so we'd have a decent view of the women when they returned from the club they were at. We wouldn't be able to miss them. Time ticked by slowly.

I sat at the edge of my seat, a beer in hand, and my eyes glued on the lobby. "How much longer do we have to wait?"

"As long as we have to." Nico leaned back comfortably in his chair and swirled his scotch around his glass. "Sit back and enjoy your beer."

I eyed Nico. To anyone else, he appeared completely at ease. After this week, I can tell he's far from relaxed. He's coiled as tight as a cobra, ready to strike. I know how he feels, but our need to rescue Roxanne is different.

"When we get Rox back." I said. "And she still wants to marry you, then I won't get in your way."

Nico looked over at me. "Thank you."

"Don't get me wrong, I'm still not your biggest fan. But the more time I've spent with you, the more I see the truth."

"What truth is that?"

"That you truly do love my sister. She's not some pawn to use as retaliation or a shield against my family."

"Never." Nico said firmly. "I love Roxanne with everything I am."

I smiled. "I am leaving her in good hands."

Giggling caught my attention. Not just any giggling, but Lexi's giggling. I'd recognize it anywhere. I turned my attention back to the lobby. *What is she doing here?* Lexi was supposed to be back in Frostham with Lucky. There was a single man with a group of four women — Lexi, Rox, Candi, and someone I didn't recognize. He had to be Andrew. Lexi was leaning heavily into Andrew, who had his arm around her waist, keeping her tightly at his side.

"Not yet." Nico gripped my wrist, holding me down in the chair. "We need to wait for him to leave the hotel."

"But." My eyes tracked Lexi and the others. "Did you know Lexi would be here?"

"I did. Candi told me that Rox insisted on it."

"That changes everything."

"No, it doesn't. All our planning has all four of them included in our exit plan."

He's right. We did plan to escape with four people. I ground my teeth. Seeing Lexi here, without knowing she'd be here, has my insides twisting. I believe our relationship is strong enough that I don't have to worry about her falling for Andrew, yet seeing her sway into his arms had a surge of jealousy sprout inside. I'm also afraid that Andrew may make a move on Lexi while she's in a drunken state. I could tell that he wanted her because of the way he was holding her. I chugged back my beer, frustrated I couldn't go to my woman right this instant.

"Okay." Nico said after a short while and finished his drink. "Let's get into position and wait for Candi."

We took the stairs up a few flights, waiting for Candi to tell us that Andrew had left before we hopped in an elevator. It was a precaution to avoid Andrew in the lobby. Nico took the lead, walking down the hall of the fifteenth floor at a brisk pace before stopping at a door. He took a moment to straighten his jacket and run fingers through his hair, hesitating before knocking.

Candi opened the door wide, relief on her face as she stepped out to hug him. "I'm so glad you're here."

"We have to be quick." Nico replied.

"Grab your bag." Candi ordered while re-entering the room. "We're moving rooms."

There were grumbles and questions from within. Rox and Lexi had no idea what was going on. Oddly enough, the fourth woman didn't say a word. In fact, the pink-haired woman took the lead, followed by Lexi, then Rox, who Candi was pushing out.

"I'm not going anywhere." Roxanne stated. "Not without Andrew."

Lexi looked at me with wide eyes. She looked absolutely stunning in a tight midnight blue dress. I didn't miss the detail of her kiss-swollen lips and flushed cheeks. I clenched my hands at my sides and narrowed my eyes at her. Lexi averted her gaze as if embarrassed. It only pissed me off even more. I wanted to demand to know what happened but now is not the time. There will be time later.

Lexi took Rox's hand. "Roxanne, in ten minutes, if you want to come back, we will."

Lexi quickly glanced at me as if hoping that Rox would never want to come back to this room. If she did, then we would have failed in our rescue. Lexi may not have known that Nico and I would be here, but she seems to have picked up on what was going on and was trying to help.

"Ten minutes." Roxanne agreed, and then her eyes found me, and fear filled them. "Tyler?"

"Let's go." Candi insisted. "Brina has the elevator open."

The pink-haired woman I now know as Brina kept the doors open. All five of us rushed to join her and crowded into the steel box. We went down two floors, with Brina taking the lead to the new room and unlocking it with a key card she miraculously had in her hand. I knew there would be a second room, but I thought Nico had booked it.

"Why is Tyler here?" Rox demanded. "Did we really need to grab our bags from our room?"

"We don't plan on going back." Brina stated while taking a seat at the desk.

"I don't understand."

"You need your memories." Candi said softly. "We don't have time for them to return gradually. Franco is imbedding himself too deeply."

"Lexi?" Rox turned to her best friend for support.

"You need your memories." Lexi confirmed. "I had nothing to do with this scheme, but I agree with the reasoning behind it."

"Roxanne." I took a step forward, and she flinched. "Why are you afraid of me?"

"You hate me." Rox said quietly, taking hold of Lexi's hand. "For marrying a Frangione."

"I don't hate you. I could never hate you." I told her.

"You don't need to lie. Franco told me that you abandoned me." She insisted. "That my parents disowned me."

Silence ensued after that statement. *How could she believe that lie?* I marched forward, determined to disprove that flimsy lie. Roxanne stumbled away from me, knees hitting the bed and falling onto it. She took Lexi down with her. I knelt, taking her hands in mine. I made sure I had her full attention before speaking again.

"Roxanne Caroline Baxter, I will always love you. You are my sister." I told her. "My frustratingly annoying little sister. Friends, family, co-workers, and your fiancée love you. The moment you went missing, we all did our best to find you."

"Tyler." Tears brimmed her eyes.

"Yes, Rox?"

"You're lying." She pulled her hands free.

"I'm not."

"You put me behind bars."

"Of course, you remember that." I groaned. "I only put you in the holding cells because you were interfering with an investigation. You were never actually charged with anything."

Roxanne stared back at me, her brows furrowing. "I was interfering with an investigation?"

"It's true." Lexi supplied. "You told me the whole story while showing off your engagement ring."

Roxanne looked down at the ring. *That ring and Nico are the keys to bringing her back to us.* I could see it in the way her eyes softened as she stared at the piece of jewellery. Nico placed a hand on my shoulder. I moved out of the way, and Rox looked up, not at me but at Nico.

"Who are you?" Roxanne asked.

"Who do you think I am?" He countered.

She tilted her head. "I've met you before, haven't I? You seem familiar."

Nico reached down, taking her hands and tugging her up onto her feet. Roxanne didn't fight him, as if too curious about who he is. An eerie silence fell upon the room as we watched, waiting with bated breath for either Roxanne to remember or for Nico's next move.

He cupped her face in his hands. "Ti amo, Bella."

I saw her eyes widen, then he leaned in and kissed my sister. I watched, transfixed, mentally praying this would be a Sleeping Beauty moment — a prince's kiss to wake the princess. *This had to work.* Roxanne struggled, slapping at his chest, trying to push him away. Nico held on, intensifying the kiss. Amazingly, my sister's struggle subsided.

"Did it work?" I whispered, afraid to break the spell.

"I don't know." Lexi whispered back. "I think so."

"It worked." Brina grinned. "She's enjoying the kiss too much for it to have not worked."

"How long are they going to keep kissing?" I grumbled.

Lexi slapped me upside the head. "Don't be a jerk."

I rubbed at the back of my head. A small smile tugged at my lips that she couldn't see. I don't know what happened earlier, but I was thankful for the subconscious gesture. *At least she doesn't hate me.*

"They'll come up for air." Candi said. "Eventually."

Finally, Nico pulled back. "Bella?"

Roxanne gripped his wrists, pulling them from her face. My hope sank. *It didn't work.* Nothing we do next will work. All of our planning has gone to waste.

"Bella?" Nico asked again, frowning.

She reached up to cup his face. "You're the dragon who would burn the world for me."

Nico smiled. "I missed you, Bella."

"Lock me up in your tower, and don't ever let me go."

"Come si desidera."

"Rox?" I stood and touched her shoulder lightly.

She turned and hugged me. "Ty."

I enveloped her in my arms. "We missed you so much."

Now that Roxanne is back, we can get out of here. Then, I can address Lexi's well-kissed state. Thinking of it still pisses me off. If Andrew forced himself on her, I was going to enjoy punching him for it. But if she engaged in the kiss or enjoyed it, I'm not sure what I'd do. I was torn between hating myself for ghosting her and hating her for being swayed by another man so quickly.

Twenty-One

LEXI

THE fire alarm sounded.

"Perfect timing." Nico took Rox's hand and her bag. "That's our cue to leave."

"It sounds like you planned this." I stated.

"The best way to get all of you out of here." Tyler said, taking my bag and pushing me forward gently before taking the lead. "We'll blend in with the rest of the hotel guests."

Smart. Candi and Brina were already moving toward the door with their bags. Nico must have shared the plan with Candi, who shared it with Brina, which is why they immediately packed today's purchases. *Why didn't Tyler tell me of the plan?* My heart tightened as I watched his back head for the stairs. *Maybe he doesn't trust me.*

Once outside the hotel, Nico and Tyler strategically moved us further away. Guests were far from happy to be woken in the middle of the night, and the children were even less happy. Sirens could be heard in the distance and getting louder as they came to deal with the alarm.

Nearly free of the crowd, someone clamped down on my wrist. Panic rose that it might be Andrew. I turned slowly to see who held my wrist. My panic morphed into disgust as I stared at Bradley.

"Let me go." I tugged at my wrist.

"First the club, now this hotel." Bradley smiled. "It must be fate, Alexis."

"Fate?" I scoffed. "It's only my bad luck."

He tugged me closer. "It's fate telling us that we're meant to be together."

An arm snaked around my waist and tugged me against a hard body. Tyler's hard body. With his other hand, he gripped Bradley's wrist. The man's face contorted in pain, and he released me.

"Let me go." Bradley hissed.

"You didn't let go of my woman when she asked." Tyler stated. "Why should I let you go?"

Bradley sneered at me. "This isn't the same guy from the club."

"My life is none of your business." I snapped, brave now that Tyler is around.

Tyler let Bradley go and turned us away from him. "Let's go."

Bradley followed, trying to get answers to his probing questions. He was drawing too much attention our way. The fire trucks had arrived at the hotel and had stolen the attention of most of the gawkers. The eyes and ears that had turned to watch the fuss Bradley was making had finally turned away.

Nico looked at his phone. "We're running out of time."

"Shit." Tyler shoved me down an alley. "Go with Nico. I'll be right behind you."

"Ty." I squeezed his forearm, making sure I had his attention. "That's my ex."

Fury blazed in his green eyes, and his jaw hardened. I may not have wanted Andrew to defend me earlier tonight but Tyler's different. I wouldn't be able to explain the difference. I only knew that it was. Nico waited at a car, hidden in the alley, with the back door open. I slid in next to Roxanne, the door closed, and Nico slid in behind the wheel.

"Where are Candi and Brina?" I asked.

"There was another car waiting for them." Rox answered.

"All part of the plan." Nico said.

I frowned. "Are you going to tell us the plan?"

The trunk slammed shut, and Tyler got in next to Nico. Nico handed him his phone. Whatever plan they had made seemed to have been memorized. Without speaking to each other, they moved forward with their plan.

Back in Frostham, Nico pulled into the garage of an ordi-
nary-looking house. Rox and I had fallen asleep on the drive.
I only woke up because I'd felt the car slow — and not in a
coming to a red light kind of slow. Rubbing my eyes with one
hand, I reached over to shake Roxanne awake.

"Ugh." She grumbled. "Where are we?"

"At a safe house." Tyler said. "Let's get you two inside."

"Why would we need a safe house?"

"For now, it's to keep you out of Franco's clutches."

Rox winced as if pained by staying away from him. We all exited the car and went inside. Nico suggested that we all take the next few hours to sleep before we get moving in the morning. *Sleep, a good sleep, sounds heavenly.* Nico took Rox's bag from the trunk, and her hand, then went upstairs.

"We should do the same." Tyler said to me. With my bag in hand, he was ready to go upstairs.

"Not yet." I took his hand and pulled him to the kitchen. "You should ice these knuckles."

"I'll be fine, Lexi."

I hesitated with my hand on the freezer door handle. "Thank you for standing up for me."

"If you're insisting on the ice, then maybe we should talk."

Tyler pulled a chair out from the kitchen table, spun it to face the kitchen, and sat down. I found an ice tray in the freezer and pulled it out. An ice pack would have been better, but this would do.

"Okay." I said softly.

"Let's start with those kiss-swollen lips of yours."

My shoulders tightened as I cracked the ice tray and dumped a few cubes into a towel. Gathering the ends to make a pouch, I handed it over to him. He was glaring at me. I could see the barely contained fury in his tight muscles.

I retreated to the kitchen, keeping as much distance between us as possible. "I was kissing Andrew."

"Why?" He ground out.

"I was told to get Andrew out of the hotel, then was shoved out of the room."

"So you kissed him. Then what? Did he leave to go get condoms?"

I pursed my lips. *How could he think that of me?*

"Lexi." His growl was a warning.

"I asked him to get me French Fries." I said defensively.

"French Fries?"

I nodded. "Andrew requested one kiss per fry. So, I grabbed his head and kissed him. The kiss got intense fast."

Tyler's glare hardened. "Did you enjoy kissing another man?"

I swallowed, wrapping my arms around myself. "I hate myself for enjoying Andrew's kiss."

Tyler went silent. I could feel the tears stinging the back of my eyes. I royally screwed up, but I couldn't keep it from him. My parents had a nasty divorce because of a secret affair. I swore I'd never keep an emotionally damaging secret from my partner, even if the truth broke us up.

"And what about your ex?" Tyler finally spoke. "He called you Alexis. Are you going to tell me that Lexi Dawson isn't your real name?"

"Alexis Monique Dawson." I elaborated. "Roxanne gave me the nickname of Lexi. I continued to use it because my real name reminds me too much of Bradley."

"Lexi suits you better." He mumbled.

I felt a sliver of hope bloom deep within my breaking heart that I had to squash. "Ty, do you not trust me?"

Wide, shocked eyes flew to mine. "Why would you ask me that?"

"I knew nothing about tonight." I hedged. "If I did, I would have handled Andrew differently."

Tyler glowered. "How would you have handled things?"

I opened my mouth to mention the condom errand he had mentioned but closed it. Tyler wouldn't appreciate it. Now that I think about it, Andrew had made it clear that he wanted me, so he probably already had condoms in his bag. That would have backfired on me pretty quickly.

"I could have overplayed being drunk and asked him to get me medication." I wiped at the few tears that managed to escape.

"You could have done that in the first place."

"I didn't think of it until now." I defended. "All I had was a shove to the hall and a suggestion of French Fries."

"Did Andrew do anything else toward you?"

"He wanted to." Fresh tears began to fall at how close I'd come to being stripped naked by Andrew. "I could feel him through his jeans, how hard he was for me."

Tyler stood and walked toward me. I kept my gaze on the floor, not watching to see the anger in his eyes. He cupped my cheek, his thumb brushing at the tears.

"I'm sorry you were put in that situation, honey." He said. "If I knew you were going to be there tonight, I would have told you the plan."

"I've been trying so hard to squash his flirting." I told him.

"Why didn't you tell me sooner?"

"I had you to run to at the end of the day." I looked up at him. "But this weekend, I had nowhere to run. And since you ghosted me, I felt alone in my battle."

"I knew going radio silent would hurt you." Tyler stepped back. "I didn't want to do it, not after last time."

"Then why do it?"

Tyler sighed, running a hand through his hair. "I've been on leave from the force pending an IA investigation."

"IA?"

"Internal affairs."

I sucked in a sharp breath. I had so many questions. But unlike him, with my explanation about Andrew, I didn't interrupt.

"Last week, Nico was arrested, and I broke him out of the station's holding cells." Tyler began to explain. "I, no we, had to go radio silent and hide. Not being able to talk to you or to explain anything killed me. Many times, I wanted to call and hear your voice when you picked up."

"That's why you ghosted me?"

"It is."

"Then why are you under investigation? And why didn't you tell me? You really don't trust me, do you?"

"That's not it." Tyler reached out, a hint of panic in his voice.

"Then, why?"

"It just never came up."

"It never came up?" I repeated a hint of hysteria in my voice.

He sighed, dropping his hand. "To sum it up, the higher-ups think I'm taking too much of the force's resources to look for

Roxanne. When I walked out, the first thing that went through my mind was that it would be good for us. We could focus on building a stronger relationship."

"Build a stronger relationship." I laughed bitterly. "In one night, we destroyed that."

"We hit a bump, that's all."

"You kept two big secrets from me, Ty. The first was about your career, and the other was about tonight."

Tyler narrowed his eyes. "You also kept Roxanne from me."

I reared back as if slapped. "You saw her tonight. If you had crossed paths with her sooner, she would have turned tail right into Franco's arms."

He winced. "You could have at least told me about my sister."

"Maybe, but it's too late now."

My heart was breaking. In one conversation, we went from being a couple to needing to break up. *If there's no trust, there's no relationship.* Walking away from Tyler is going to be damaging to my emotions. He's been the one I've wanted for over three years.

"What are you saying, Lexi?"

"Maybe I deleted my dating apps too soon." My voice clogged with tears.

Fury made Tyler's green eyes brighten. "You are not running away from me, Lexi."

"You don't trust me, Ty. Maybe I'm not the right woman for you if you can't trust me."

"You couldn't be more wrong."

Tyler kissed me with all the emotion he wanted to convey. Tears flowed freely as I melted into him. I felt his love for me in this kiss. I will give him tonight, our last night together, but after that, it's over.

They say if you love something, then set it free. Whoever 'they' are, they never said how hard it is to do that. In this case, it has to be done. Tyler needs to find a woman that he trusts enough to tell her everything. I don't know what I need, but I know I need time to figure that out.

Breaking up with Tyler is the hardest thing I've ever had to do.

Twenty-Two

TYLER

WHEN I WOKE UP, Lexi wasn't lying next to me. I sat up, looked around the room and noted that her bag was gone, too. In my frustration, I punched the mattress. *Damn it. She really is running.* There was only a sliver of hope that I could convince her otherwise if I took her to bed. But since she's not here, it didn't work.

I really didn't handle her right yesterday. When she confessed to kissing another man, I felt betrayed. Even if the circumstances were to get him out of the hotel so Nico and I wouldn't get caught taking Roxanne away. I thought I had Lexi's heart. Guess not. Our sexual chemistry is explosive, and our date at the fair was fantastic. What more can I give her to convince her that she's it for me?

Trust. She stated as much last night. I did trust her. I trusted her not to fall for Andrew. I trusted that she'll always be mine. *At least she didn't fall for Andrew.*

I didn't tell her about the IA investigation because it's a load of bull, and it pissed me off. She didn't need to know that she was in a relationship with a jobless man. When it came to Roxanne's rescue after Nico had been broken from jail, all the finer details were set in place. I didn't want Lexi to get caught in any crossfire.

"I should have told her everything." I mumbled to myself. "I should have called. I could have called."

It really is my fault. Without realizing I was pushing her away emotionally, I had lost Lexi. I need to make it up to her. I need her back. It's only been a few hours without Lexi, and I'm already an emotional mess. Lexi may have let me go, but I haven't let her go. Not without a fight.

I got out of bed and ran through the shower. Today, Nico and I will deal with Franco, then I can focus on Lexi. At the top of the stairs, I heard my sister squeal in delight.

"I can't believe you did that." Rox exclaimed.

"It happened." Lexi replied.

I froze at the top, wanting to hear what they were talking about.

"Well, come on, I need details." Rox prompted. "How was the kiss with Andrew? You initiated it this time, right?"

"I did, but only as a lure to get him out of the hotel."

The hurt of the betrayal weighed down my heart. I didn't want to hear her talk about the kiss with Andrew, so I stomped down the steps to ensure they knew I was coming. Maybe the breakup will be good for us, and then we can come back stronger. Or it could destroy us both.

"Morning." I said when I hit the bottom.

"Tyler." Rox whined. "Go help Nico in the kitchen. You're interrupting our girl talk."

I looked past Rox to Lexi. She wasn't even looking at me. *Are those tears in her eyes?* I wanted to wrap her in my arms and tell her I'm not going anywhere. But I can't, not right now. We need to get Roxanne home and Franco out of her life for good first. Then, and only then, will I haul Lexi over my shoulder and handcuff her to my bed. With nowhere to go, she'll be forced to listen.

"Good morning, Tyler." Nico greeted me when I entered the kitchen. "Would you like some pancakes?"

I blinked. "I didn't know you could cook."

"Only pancakes."

I couldn't hear Lexi and Roxanne's conversation. I swear they lowered their voices so neither of us could hear.

"What can I do to help?" I asked.

Nico looked around at the ingredients he'd used for the batter. "You can put everything away, then set the table."

"Will do."

I started my task. "So, how was Roxanne last night?"

"What do you mean, exactly?"

"After all the hecticness of getting out of Alexo, how are her memories?"

Nico let out a frustrated sound. "They are still jumbled."

"How so?"

"Anything related to Dagger Designs and Lexi is intact." He explained. "That's the good news. The bad news is that she cried out for Franco last night. It took me a while to remind her who I am."

I placed glasses and cutlery on the table. "Do you think we should go with Plan P?"

Nico flipped the pancakes. "I think Plan J will be better."

Plan P involves contacting Jaylen. He had a relationship with Rox, and because it was older than the one she had with Nico, it might have done something to her memory. I wasn't sure if it would remind her of her time with my partner, which could have her fall back into that relationship, or if she would remember breaking up with him and then wind up leaning more toward Nico.

Nico filled the plates with pancakes, calling out to the girls. "Breakfast."

They came in, arms looped with each other and sat down. Nico grabbed orange juice before taking a seat next to Roxanne. I took the seat next to Lexi, who seemed to shrink away from me. We were all silent around the table as we began to eat.

"Did you put cinnamon in these?" Roxanne asked.

"Sì." Nico smiled at her.

There was a strange expression on her face as she examined a piece of pancake on her fork. "You made these for me for breakfast after our first night together."

"That's right, Bella."

She fell silent, and we all continued to eat. It was good to hear her remember something.

"Franco kissed me for the first time that night, too. Didn't he?" Rox inquired.

"He did." Nico ground his teeth. "But you retaliated, furious and disgusted with him."

"Then why did I marry him?"

"You didn't." Lexi explained, lifting Roxanne's hand. "This ring was given to you by the one you chose to marry."

Rox smiled at the ring. "I love this ring."

"And you love the man who gave it to you."

"Nico." She said slowly. "Nico gave me this ring."

"That's right."

Roxanne's memories are a mess. It seems that after some sleep, a cloud fell over them again. I could see the struggle she was having sorting through the jumbled mess. Thankfully, Lexi is here. Nico is right. The only person that Roxanne clearly remembers and believes is Lexi.

"Ty?"

I looked over at my sister. "Yes, Rox?"

"Why are you here? Shouldn't you be at work?"

"I took time off to find you."

Lexi flicked a quick look my way before returning to Roxanne. "See? I told you he'd never abandon you."

Rox gave a little nod. "Family is important."

Nico slid the burner phone over to me. "Make the call to activate Plan J, and I'll clean up. Bella, Lexi, we'll be leaving in twenty minutes."

Lexi frowned but didn't argue. She wanted to, though. She wanted to know the details of Plan J. Instead, she took Roxanne by the hand and led her back upstairs. I went to the garage to make the call, so it wasn't overheard. I don't want Rox to panic like she did when she saw me yesterday.

The phone rang twice before it was answered. "Hello?"

"Jenna, I do hope I didn't catch you at a bad time." I said, as a precaution.

"Just give me a moment." She said.

I could hear her telling someone not to record or listen in as this was a private conversation. Someone was arguing against her, and that person wound up losing. No one could win against her in an argument. *Way to go, Prosecutor Mom.*

"Okay." Mom came back on the line. "I apologize for the delay."

"I need you to meet me in forty-five minutes."

"Yes, of course. If you have an earlier appointment, then I'll take it."

I rattled off an address that's in an impoverished part of Frostham. "Be careful."

"Yes. Thank you for your call."

With that, the call ended. It's a good thing I was cautious. The house phone was set up to record me calling home. Clearly, Dad thought I'd call Mom at some point while I was in hiding. He wasn't wrong.

"It's all set up." I announced, returning the phone to Nico.

"Good. She'll be there?" He confirmed.

"In forty-five minutes."

This will give Mom enough time to lose whatever tail is going to be following her. I have no doubt Dad would have her followed as a precautionary backup to the recorded phone. We won't avoid the cops forever. I'll put the battery back in my phone when the time is right. They'll come rushing in and, if all goes well, arrest Franco.

Twenty-Three

LEXI

NICO AND TYLER DROVE us to an impoverished part of Frostham. The housing was dilapidated. Squatters and addicts of all kinds occupied most dwellings. *This city really needs to do something about this.* It was disgusting to see, but it also broke my heart that there are citizens who are barely living in this area.

"Why are we here?" I asked in a hushed whisper.

"A precaution for what's to come." Tyler answered.

"It's not ideal." Nico continued. "But necessary."

The car was parked in the garage. Tyler took us inside and swept the house to ensure it was clear of people. Nico waited in the garage. Clearly, someone was supposed to meet us here.

"I don't like it here." Rox said, clinging to me.

"Me neither." I admitted, clinging to her.

I looked around the space. Windows were broken, cabinets were falling off their hinges, and there were even cracks in the outside walls. Dust covered the surfaces in thick piles, and cobwebs decorated every corner. It seemed like forever before there was the sound of another car. Then, Nico walked into the house with Jenna Baxter.

"Mom?" Rox ran to her.

Jenna hugged her daughter tightly. "Oh, sweetheart."

I didn't know what was happening. "Why are you here, Jenna?"

"Tyler called me this morning. He gave me this address and a time."

"Mom." Rox pulled back. "Did you disown me?"

Jenna took her face in her hands. "Never. We love you too much."

"Franco told me I was disowned."

"Franco is a liar and a criminal. He took you from us by force."

"So, I didn't marry Franco?" Roxanne asked again.

"No, sweetheart." Jenna kissed her forehead. "You're happily engaged to Nico."

Roxanne hugged her. "I want to go home."

"Excellent idea." A male voice said.

I spun to see a man with dark eyes and dark hair. If it wasn't for the angular features and broader shoulders, then I might have mistaken him for Nico. *This has to be Franco.*

"Come, Farfalla." He beckoned with an outstretched hand.

"Roxanne isn't going anywhere with you." Tyler stepped forward with a gun in hand.

Where did he get that? He'd put on his cop face as he levelled the gun at Franco.

Franco smiled, unfazed. "You're not going to shoot me. Even without the badge, you're still a cop at heart."

"I'm also a protective big brother."

"It's over, Franco." Nico declared.

I glanced over. Nico had put himself between Franco and Roxanne. Jenna still held her daughter tightly and slowly moved them backward, putting the wall at her back. Panic began to climb up my spine. From where I stood, I was completely exposed. Instinct had me wanting to run and hide behind Tyler, but common sense kept me in place so as not to distract him.

"It's far from over, little brother." Franco sneered. "Roxanne is my wife, and soon we'll rule the Frangione empire together."

"She's not your wife." Nico spat.

"I have the marriage certificate that says otherwise." He smiled.

"Ah yes, that piece of paper that's easily forged." Nico smiled. "What a shame the priest who certified it is dead."

"A tragedy." Franco agreed.

"Taking my fiancée was your biggest mistake."

Franco frowned. "What are you talking about?"

"You've been so preoccupied with keeping her memory loss intact and keeping her away from me that you haven't noticed that I was tearing down the empire you were creating." Nico said far too calmly. "It took time, but I managed to break it down. I also have the doctor who kept Roxanne in a coma, and he's willing to testify against you."

"Let's not forget the man who kidnapped Roxanne in the first place." Tyler added.

"You have nothing on me." Franco smiled again.

"That's where you're wrong. Enzo has surprisingly given the police a helping hand. He handed over the information on the cigar-smoking man, the man you would have ordered to have my sister end up in some non-fatal accident. Pretty soon, he'll be arrested for kidnapping and murder."

Franco narrowed his eyes. "I highly doubt that."

"Patrick Mann was the first to be arrested." Tyler said with satisfaction. "That way, he couldn't warn you of what was to come."

Franco's face somehow hardened and flared with fury all at the same time. It was frightening. The room went entirely silent as three powerful and dangerous men stood there waiting for the next move. I've never really thought of Tyler as dangerous before. But today, in this dilapidated house, while holding a gun steady at the man who forcefully took his sister away, he's dangerous. Yet, I wasn't frightened of him.

Roxanne gasped, breaking the tense silence. I shifted, following her scared, wide eyes to a beefy man. He held a gun steady at Tyler's back, a cigar in his mouth. He reached up to remove the cigar before speaking.

"Put down the gun." His harsh voice, full of authority, said. "Slowly."

"Who are you going to shoot if I don't?" Tyler questioned the man.

"Does it matter?"

Tyler hesitated for a breath before raising both hands in the air and removing his finger from the trigger. Slowly, he bent down and placed the gun on the ground before standing back up. Finally, he kicked the gun away. At least he kicked it in a direction away from everyone else in the room.

"Now, Mr. Frangione is going to take his wife home." The man announced. "Before you argue, my men have this place surrounded."

A red dot appeared on my chest.

"Tyler." I whispered, staring down at it.

Tyler looked over at me, his eyes going wide. "Lexi."

"How convenient." The cigar man snickered. "You just made my job easier."

"My wife." Franco warned.

"Mrs. Frangione." The man turned his head to Roxanne. "If you'd be so kind as to join Mr. Frangione."

Roxanne looked on, her eyes wide with fear. Jenna held her daughter tighter. Nico inched over to prevent Rox from moving. The man clicked his tongue, moved his gun from Tyler and fired at Nico before returning the gun to Tyler. Rox cried out at the gunshot. Nico gripped his shoulder, his face twisting in agony. I covered my mouth to prevent a scream from escaping.

"Now, Mrs. Frangione, if you would please comply." The cigar man prompted.

Tears rolled down Rox's face as she pulled away from her mom. Jenna tried to hold on, but Rox peeled her off so she could go to Franco.

"Bella, don't." Nico pleaded, reaching for her as she walked by.

"I have to." She replied softly.

Franco took her by the upper arm. "Let's go home, Farfalla."

I watched in horror as Franco took Roxanne away. *This can't be happening.* We were so close to getting Rox back home with her family and Nico. Was Franco showing up part of the plan? I wouldn't know since Tyler didn't trust me enough to tell me anything important.

Sirens could be heard in the distance, and they were getting closer. Things erupted into chaos. Tyler, bolstered by the sound, roared with rage, shoving the cigar man back. Nico grabbed the gun Tyler had abandoned and raced out of the house. I rushed over to Jenna. I felt safe in her arms, even with everything going on around us.

Gunshots began to fire both in the house and outside. I screamed. Jenna covered my head as debris broke off and flew around. *Tyler. Where is Tyler?* I looked over to where I'd last seen him. He wasn't there. I inched away from Jenna, desperate to find him.

Tyler and the cigar man had moved their fight to a front room, which was void of most furniture except a couch and chair, which were pushed against the walls. Fists flew between the two men as they fought. Landing punches to the face and gut. Elbows and feet were not excluded from the fight. Soon, the cigar man had the apparent upper hand when a punch sent Tyler to the ground. *Get up!* I mentally shouted. Tyler struggled to get to his knees, and the man kicked him back down.

Cigar man then went for the gun that was lost in their hand-to-hand fight. Time seemed to slow as he aimed the gun at Tyler. I got to my feet, running at the beefy man, wanting to save Tyler. The gun went off.

Twenty-Four

TYLER

IT'S BEEN A WEEK, and Lexi still hasn't woken up.

I've never felt fear like the fear I felt watching Lexi charge at the cigar man to protect me. However, she had stumbled, and instead of knocking into the man, she tumbled into the bullet path. I crawled over to her, pulled off my shirt and pressed it to her side. Cops came in to arrest him, and an ambulance was called for Lexi.

I rode with her to the hospital, where she was taken in for immediate surgery. The bullet was retrieved, and the doctors were able to stop the bleeding. The doctors said her body went into shock, but with some rest, she'll be just fine. They'll keep her under watch while she recovers. When I knew she was going to be all right, Dad took me to the station to give my report of the events while Mom stayed by Lexi's side for me.

I started by explaining my reasoning behind breaking Nico out of the holding cell. Then, I explained how we protected the doctor who kept Rox in a coma, found the evidence against Patrick Mann, and tore down Franco's empire. That part was easier than I thought it would be. All we had to do was slide some information to Enzo's men, and they did all the work. It also helped that Nico did a lot of the work in the month prior.

Nico had successfully saved Roxanne from Franco. Much to Dad's displeasure, she stayed by his side while he recovered in the hospital. Nico's report of the events was similar to mine, which kept him out of jail. Roxanne's testimony, along with that of the doctor, will keep Franco in prison for a very long time. That inconvenient marriage certificate was proven to be a forgery, which made Nico and Rox extraordinarily relieved.

I had my badge returned to me, clear of whatever charges Patrick Mann was accusing me of that had sent internal affairs after me in the first place. The station was being cleaned up of anyone on the Frangione payroll. Things were starting to go back to normal. All I need is for Lexi to wake up so I can fix things with her.

"Ty, I know you're thankful that Lexi saved your life." Jaylen stopped by for a visit and handed me a cup of coffee. "But it's been a week. Are you really going to sit here and wait for her to wake up to say thank you?"

"It's more than that."

"What do you mean?" He took a seat in the chair on the opposite side of Lexi.

I looked down at her, asleep in the bed, machines monitoring her life force. "I love her."

"Love? All because she saved your life?"

"It's more than that." I repeated.

Jaylen looked down at Lexi, then back up at me, his eyes widening with sudden understanding. "She's the woman from the bar three years ago."

I didn't answer. There was no need. Now that he knows, things started to fall into place in his mind. I know my partner well enough to recognize his look when all the evidence in one of our cases falls into place. That's the same look he has now.

"Why didn't you tell me?" He asked.

"Lexi." I said, swallowing back a lump in my throat. "It's because of Lexi that I didn't say anything."

A raised brow from Jaylen indicated he didn't understand. I took a moment to sort through my mind on the best possible way to explain. As far as I know, he hasn't been in love, so he may not understand even after I explain.

"At first, Lexi was only comfortable with a sex-only relationship. I had to convince her that I wanted more, that she was safe with me." I provided the most straightforward and briefest explanation. "I stayed quiet about her because that's what she wanted. Because she wasn't comfortable announcing our relationship to the world yet."

Jaylen shook his head. "I don't get it."

"You didn't say anything about you and Roxanne when you were sleeping with her." I countered.

"That part I understand." He grimaced. "It's the part about keeping the relationship a secret when it grew beyond sex only."

"I didn't think you would. One day, though, you will."

"I thought Roxanne would be the one for me."

I raised a brow. "Thought?"

"I still love her." He admitted, slouching in the chair. "But seeing her this week and hearing everything that happened. It hurt coming to terms with the fact that she loves Nico. Even with her memory loss, he was the one able to jog her memory."

"Love is powerful."

Jaylen's phone rang. "Parry."

I drank my coffee and watched my partner stand. A new case must have come in. I may have my badge back, but I took vacation time to be by Lexi's side until she woke up. I want to be the first face that she sees.

"I hope Lexi wakes up soon." Jaylen clapped my shoulder. "I could really use my partner back at the station."

"I hope she wakes up soon, too."

Jaylen left, and I was alone with Lexi and all the steadily beeping machines. The doctors are optimistic since her recovery has been going well with all the rest. After what happened to Roxanne, I'm a little fearful she might not remember our relationship. I got up to throw the empty coffee cup into the garbage.

"Wake up soon, Lexi." I returned to her side, taking her hand and kissing her forehead. "I need you in my life. I love you, Lexi Dawson."

Suddenly, the machines started to go wild. I stepped back, calling for a doctor. Medical staff came rushing in, pushing me aside so they could tend to her. *Please be okay.* I moved as far back as the door as I watched them.

"Ty, what's going on?" Roxanne slipped into the room, her hand squeezing my arm as she stared at the medical team.

I placed my hand on top of hers. "I'm not sure."

A gasp of air cut through all the noise, and I thought my knees were going to buckle with relief. Lexi was awake. I could hear her asking questions while the staff checked her over. Slowly, they filtered out so Rox and I could get closer.

"Rox!" Lexi cried out, her arms outstretched. "Oh my God. I wasn't sure I'd see you again."

Roxanne hugged her best friend. "I could say the same thing. You've been out for a week."

Her eyes found mine. "You're okay."

Unable to resist, I cupped her face and kissed her. "Don't you dare frighten me like that ever again, honey."

She pushed me back. "I thought that cigar man was going to kill you."

"Then throw something at the shooter. Anything but yourself."

She nodded.

"Did you two hook up while I was in a coma?" Rox asked.

"We're not together." Lexi teared up. "Not anymore."

"Oh."

Nothing more could be said. I stumbled back as the girls hugged. I hoped she'd forget about breaking up with me. Her rejection hurt. She wouldn't even look at me. *Did I lose her forever?*

"I'm glad she's awake." Nico said softly.

I turned to see him in the small hospital room, leaning against the wall next to the door. His arm was still in a sling, and it would be for a while. At least the bullet was a through-and-through. There will be a scar, but that's minor.

"Yeah." I jerked my chin to his shoulder. "Any damage?"

"It was clean." He confirmed.

"Thanks again for saving Roxanne."

Nico shook his head. "There's no need to thank me. I would have saved her no matter what."

I looked back over at Lexi. Roxanne was sitting on the tiny bed with her. She had an arm wrapped around her as Lexi sat there with her face buried in her hands. They weren't talking, yet they sat there as if everything had already been said.

"Should we give them some space?" Nico asked.

I hesitated but nodded. "I'll grab something from the cafeteria for Lexi."

The hospital cafeteria was two floors down. Nico and I made the trek, at least to the elevator, in comfortable silence.

"So, you and Lexi?" He asked. "How long has that been going on?"

"Three years in the making." I answered. Something about Nico made me compelled to answer. "She pushed me away, but when Rox was kidnapped and I spent more time with her, it felt like a second chance."

"So you're serious about her?"

"Very much so." I glanced at him. "Why?"

Nico's lips twitched. "She's a loyal guard dog."

It took me a moment. "You had a call from Loyal Guard Dog. Was that Lexi?"

"Yep."

"Why do you call her that?"

The cafeteria was half-full. I could see medical staff having a bite to eat and a few visitors who looked like they may have been at the hospital for hours, just like me. I bought a bag of chips, an apple, a wrap, and a water bottle and went to sit. I can eat half the wrap now and offer the other half to Lexi if she'd like it. Nico had bought a water bottle, opening it with some difficulty but succeeding on his own.

"When I was trying to find out some information on Roxanne, Lexi would refuse to give me the answers. She protected Roxanne, and I ended up calling her a Loyal Guard Dog."

"That sounds like Lexi." I smiled. "About Roxanne."

Nico frowned. "What about her?"

"I know I wasn't too thrilled about the two of you, but she chose a decent man."

"Thanks, Tyler."

"If you break her heart, though, I will put your ass in jail."

He laughed. Nico Frangione won't be too bad of a brother-in-law.

"What happened between you and Lexi?"

"After returning to Alexo, she broke up with me."

Nico raised a brow. "And you accepted that?"

"Hell no." I scoffed.

"Good. Roxanne almost walked out on me." He confided. "But we talked it out, and I convinced her to stay."

"I didn't know that."

"Franco told her some things that I never wanted her to know. The truth hurt her, so I explained how I really feel about her." He took a breath. "In my explanation, she found out that Enzo was my father. I told her to go, not wanting to hurt her even more than I already have."

"But she stayed."

He nodded. "She didn't forgive me but was willing to let me try to get back into her good graces."

I frowned. "Why are you telling me all of this?"

"Because, if it's meant to be, like Roxanne and myself, you two will find your way back to each other."

"Lexi doesn't think I trust her." I ran a hand over my face. "I do trust her. It's just that I was trying to keep her safe by not telling her some things."

"Did you tell her that?"

"Not in so many words."

"Well, that's your first problem to fix."

I looked at him. "She also kissed Andrew. I know the reason behind it, but I still felt betrayed."

Nico winced. "That's a whole different problem."

"I want to talk things out, fix things, but she's not letting me."

"Maybe the best thing to do is to tell her everything, tell her the truth behind the secrets, then give her space. Like I said before, if it's meant to be, she will come back to you."

I never expected Nico to be the one with the sage words. Everything he said hit home.

We returned to Lexi's room and found it empty except for Rox, who sat waiting in a chair.

"Where's Lexi?" I asked.

"The doctor wanted to run some tests." Rox said. "It shouldn't take long."

"Okay."

"You should go home, Ty."

I frowned at my sister. "Why?"

"Lexi told me everything." She came over and placed a hand over my heart. "Give her time to realize what she let go of."

"Time will work against me." I gripped her hand.

"Then let her know you'll always be there, but you have to walk away." Roxanne kissed my cheek. "Trust that she'll find her way back to you."

Nico reminded Rox of the meeting she had with Barbara. She went to him, leaving me along with my thoughts. I sat down and waited for the doctor to bring Lexi back. I don't want to let Lexo go, but both Nico and Roxanne are telling me to do just that. *If I hold on, am I hurting her more than if I let go?* I know I'll be hurting myself.

Twenty-Five

LEXI

ALL OF MY TESTS came back good. The doctor wanted to see me again in two weeks for a check-up. Aside from that, I was able to go home. Tyler was waiting for me in the hospital room.

"Do you want me to drive you home?" He asked.

I considered a taxi, then thought better of it. "Sure, thanks."

Tyler was silent all the way home. He helped carry my bag up to my apartment, and that was it.

"Lexi, I want you to know that I do trust you." He said, staring down at me. "I kept things from you because I thought I was keeping you safe. I understand that you need time, so if you need anything, I'm only a phone call away."

With that, he kissed my cheek and walked away. My heart broke even further, and I felt tears stinging my eyes. A small part of me hoped he'd fight to keep us together, yet a larger part was relieved he was letting me go.

I almost reached out to him to stop him from going but stopped myself. *This is the right thing for us, the right thing for me.* I picked up my bag and emptied it into my hamper. The bear he'd won for me at the fair sat in the corner of my bedroom. Not wanting to be reminded of Tyler and what I had let go of, I stuffed him in my closet and took my full hamper to the building's laundry facilities. The gunshot I had sustained was mainly healed, but it was still a tender spot as I walked.

I kept myself busy for the next two days so my mind didn't wander to Tyler. I broke it off, so it shouldn't hurt this badly. Maybe it's because I had fallen in love with him. I returned home from work to find Andrew outside my apartment door with a vase of flowers.

"Andrew, what are you doing here?" I narrowed my eyes at him.

"I heard you were shot." He held up the flowers. "And recently got out of the hospital."

"I was shot by one of Franco's goons."

"I'm sorry. When Mr. Frangione heard I'd let his wife get taken, I was benched and taught a lesson."

"She wasn't his wife." I countered, unlocking my door.

"I know." He said. "It was just a job, and I was following orders. My men and I no longer work for him."

I eyed Andrew. His face looked like it was healing from a beating. Really not looking forward to another night alone, I opened my door wider. *He can offer me mind-numbing sex.* I was sure that Andrew could fulfill the request without question.

"Would you like to come in?"

He smiled and stepped into my apartment. "Thank you."

"I'm glad you're here. I wanted to apologize." I put my purse down in the kitchen.

"Apologize for what?" He placed the flowers on the kitchen counter.

"In Alexo, I was drunk when I kissed you."

"You didn't appear drunk." His lips quirked upward.

"I'm just that good of an actress." I stepped closer.

"Then, why didn't you stay? Those French Fries would have sobered you up nicely."

"At the time, I was in a relationship."

He raised a brow. "You used the past term of was. Does that mean you're no longer in that relationship?"

I nodded. "I'm single."

"So, that means I can do this."

Andrew gripped the back of my neck and kissed me. I wrapped my arms around his neck and pressed my body into him. I opened my mouth, an invitation for him to deepen the kiss. Andrew gripped my ass and lifted me onto the counter. I reached down for the hem of his shirt, tugging it upward. He pulled back to fling it over his head and pulled my shirt up over mine. Then he returned to kissing me.

Nothing was holding me back this time. The spark between us quickly fanned into an inferno. Our hands were all over each other. He unhooked my bra and played with my breasts.

I wrapped my legs around his waist and ground into him. Andrew trailed his lips down my neck, angling me backward so my breasts were arched upward for him to claim. I was aching to have him inside me.

"You're not going to kick me out and lock the door, are you?" Andrew asked when my hands went for the button on his jeans.

"There's a box of condoms in the bedroom. In the side table, along with a bottle of lube." I responded.

With a feral-sounding growl, he pulled me off the counter and carried me to the bedroom. He pulled the sheets back and laid me down. Andrew removed my jeans, then his own, before crawling on top of me. His lips found mine while his fingers played with me, stretching me and preparing me for his entrance.

"Andrew." I begged.

He reached over to the side table and pulled out a condom. Rolling it on, he returned to my mouth and slid his cock inside my opening. I cried out in ecstasy into his mouth. It felt good having him buried inside. Andrew pumped hard and fast, a frenzied reaction to the build-up that started in the kitchen. *This is what I need right now.* My orgasm came hard. Andrew pulled out and went to the attached bathroom to grab the waste bin, then returned to swap out condoms.

"How many orgasms can you handle?" Andrew crawled back onto the bed.

"Only one way to find out."

He smiled before kissing me. Andrew pulled four more orgasms out of me throughout the night. Exhausted, he cleaned me up, laid next to me, and pulled the sheets over us. I fell asleep feeling numb. The sex was fantastic, mind-blowing even, but that's all it was. Just sex. That is precisely what I want from Andrew.

I was woken by an oral orgasm to rival… I couldn't even think of what to compare this to. Andrew spent the entire day with me, naked. Aside from eating to replenish our energy, our mouths were used on each other's bodies. I found a foreign dark romance movie on a streaming network and tried to watch it with Andrew. Didn't work. We ended up having sex on the couch with the movie playing in the background. Throughout his exploration of my body, he found that secret spot inside me, that sweet spot that had me seeing stars and saying yes every time he hit it. And he took full advantage.

"Come with me to Europe." Andrew said, running fingers down my spine and following the path with his mouth.

"Europe? What brought that up?" I looked over my shoulder at him.

"My team and I have been hired to protect some rich man's daughter." He explained. "I think she's a model going on tour."

"I can't leave Frostham. I have a life here, a career, and other responsibilities."

Andrew reached for a fresh condom, then rolled onto his back and pulled me with him. He sheathed himself in the condom before empaling me onto him. Holding my hips, he adjusted me until he hit that sweet spot. I gasped, throwing my head back. To add to the pleasure, he slowly rubbed his thumb over my clit.

"I want you with me, Lexi." He said huskily. "This will never have to stop."

"Yes. Oh God, yes." My breathing quickened, lost in the pleasure. "Take me, Andrew. Take me with you."

"Music to my ears."

With his cock pressing on that sweet spot inside and his thumb continuing its rubbing, my orgasm built. Higher and higher I went until I couldn't hold back anymore. I came with Andrew's name on my lips. He didn't let me come down from the high. With tiny thrusts so that every time he hit that sweet spot, a new orgasm rose within me.

"Andrew!" I screamed.

He flipped me onto my back and kissed me. "I love it when you scream my name, Lexi."

He rode me until he came with me. Andrew cleaned me up and tucked me into his side. With the high winding down, I realized what I had agreed to.

"Andrew, I have a doctor's appointment in two weeks that I can't miss." I said, hoping it might deter him.

He kissed my shoulder. "Then, come with me for the two weeks and return for your appointment. When that's done, I'll arrange to fly you back to me."

Should I even be contemplating this? I couldn't help but think it over. After two weeks in Europe, having sex with a man who knew how to pleasure me sounded divine. Except, it sounds too much like what Franco did to Roxanne. The only difference is that I have all my faculties, and if I go, it's of my own free will. *Europe might even heal my heart.*

"Okay." I agreed. "Two weeks, then I have the option to stay here in Frostham after my appointment."

"You'll love every minute of it, Lexi, I promise."

"When do we leave?"

"Tomorrow night."

I stepped out of the hospital, stunned by the news I was given. Numbly, I made my way to Tyler's place. It's been so long I wasn't sure how to face him. *What will he say when I tell him?* Not yet ready to knock on the door, I turned and sat on the front step. A cold fall breeze blew by, and I shivered, drawing in on myself to stay warm. A bark drew my attention to the driveway. Lucky came running up to me.

"Hey, boy." I smiled, scrunching his cheeks while he tried to lick my face. "It's good to see you too."

"Do you want to come in?" Tyler asked.

"If you don't mind." I said.

Tyler unlocked his house, and I followed him inside. I removed my shoes and hung up my coat.

"Coffee?" He asked.

"No thanks." I shook my head.

"Hot chocolate then?"

"Sure."

I took a seat at the kitchen table and looked around. It looked like he had been neglecting his place. There was dust on the floor, cobwebs forming in corners, and dishes piled in the sink. The only spot taken care of was Lucky's food and water dish. *At least he isn't neglecting his dog.* Tyler took a seat at the table, placing a mug in front of me. I wrapped my hands around it and took a good look at him. He looked like he hadn't slept in weeks, and there was a scruffy beard growing along his jaw.

"How have you been?" He asked, starting up the conversation.

"Okay." I said. "How about you?"

"I could be better." He looked so sad when he said that.

"Busy with work?"

He nodded. "It's the only thing that's getting me out of bed in the mornings. You're looking good."

"Thanks." I mumbled, taking a sip of hot chocolate.

"What have you been up to?"

"Andrew asked me to go with him to Europe." I told him.

He sucked in a sharp breath. Lucky came to sit next to me. His head leaned against my leg, and I reached down to pet him. The action was comforting for what I needed to tell Tyler.

"So, you've moved on." Tyler said harshly. "With him."

I shook my head. "I did agree to go, but I made it as far as the airport. That was two weeks ago."

"You stayed." He said, sounding as if he was relieved.

"I did. The two days I had with Andrew before he left were great, but they were empty." I caught his eyes. "I thought Europe might help heal my heart, but I was wrong. Andrew tried to convince me to walk through security with him, and he almost succeeded, but I couldn't do it. I wouldn't be able to mend my heart if part of it stayed here in Frostham. So, these past two weeks helped me to figure out what I really need and want in my life."

Tyler remained silent.

"My needs and wants line up. I want more than a sexual connection. I need to feel satisfied." I took a deep breath. "Everything I had with you is exactly what I'm missing."

"Lexi." He said my name softly.

"I made a mistake letting you go, Tyler. Regret it, actually." I told him. "But I completely understand if I royally screwed up and missed my chance with you."

Tyler pushed his chair back and knelt in front of me. "I never wanted to let you go."

"Why didn't you fight for me, then?" I had to know.

"I started to, but you pushed me away." He admitted. "When I was ready to go all in, Roxanne and Nico both told me to let you go."

I sucked in a sharp breath. *He listened to them.* That was a huge chance he was taking. I could have easily not realized my mistake of letting him go. I could have gone to Europe and started a new life with Andrew.

"They said you needed time." He continued. "Time I was reluctant to give you."

"But you did it anyway."

"I had to trust that you'll find your way back to me."

Tears filled my eyes. "Thank you."

He reached up, brushing his thumb along my cheek. "Why are you crying?"

"I'm just so relieved." I pulled his hand away. "There's more I have to say. But I need to confirm something first."

He frowned, settling himself on the ground. "What is it?"

"Are we back together?"

"I want to be. I want to pretend that the last two weeks have never happened. No, like the last three weeks never happened." He said. "You breaking up with me never happened, agreed?"

"We can't do that, Ty. What happened to us, happened, and it can't be forgotten." I smiled down at him. "As long as we're together now, that's all that matters."

"I'm never letting you go again. Next time, if you threaten to walk away, I will handcuff you to my bed."

"Agreed. Now, I need to tell you about my check-up with the doctor today."

"Is everything okay? Did you get an infection?" Concerned, he reached to lift my shirt to examine the bullet wound himself.

I stopped him. "I'm pregnant."

"Pregnant?" He repeated, confused.

"About six weeks along." I told him, placing a hand over my abdomen.

"Pregnant." Tyler repeated, a smile forming on his face, and he placed his hand over mine. "With my child. No, with our child."

"So, you're happy about this?"

"Ecstatic." Tyler stood, leaned in and kissed me. "How could I not be? I have you back in my life, and we have a child forming in your body."

"Ty?"

"Yes, honey?"

"Will you take me on a date?"

"I'll take you on one every damned week." He lifted me into his arms. "In fact, I think we should recreate our first date. Which happens to be the first night I brought you home from the bar over three years ago."

I laughed, kissing him. "There's something about that night I haven't told you about."

He carried me up to his room. "Which is?"

"When you told me you were a detective, I had images of being handcuffed to the bed."

"Works out perfectly for me." Arousal lit his green eyes, and he placed me on the ground. "Now, strip and get on that bed so I can fulfill your fantasy."

With a giggle, I obeyed his command. Tyler pulled two ties from his closet, wrapping them around my wrist, then took the handcuffs from his bedside drawer and closed them overtop of the ties. He had threaded the handcuffs through a slat in his headboard, which kept my arms over my head.

"Is that okay? Does anything hurt?" He asked.

I tugged, testing to see if anything rubbed. "I'm good."

"Good." He stripped out of his clothes and crawled on top of me. "Now, I'm going to make love to you, then you're going to agree to move in with me."

Tyler did so much more than make love to me. He made me whole again. When he freed me of the handcuffs, I pushed him onto his back and lowered myself onto his cock. I introduced Tyler to that sweet spot hidden inside me. With a wicked grin, he used it to his advantage and asked me to marry him. I said yes. Over and over again. I repeated the word later when he wrapped me in his arms before we fell asleep.

About the Author

Ivy Marie grew up an army brat. Moving every two or three years, and finally settling in Ottawa, Ontario, Canada. When she's not writing she's at work, or spending time with her friends.

Both friends and family are supportive of her creative expression. She's found comfort in Supernatural Romance, with werewolves and vampires as the main creatures she writes about, and also in Contemporary Romance.

Ivy Marie writes for her own enjoyment. She also hopes that the joy she feels while writing is expressed and passed on to you.

Connect

I really appreciate you reading my book! Here are my social media coordinates;

Facebook: www.facebook.com/IvysStolenHearts
Instagram: ivymariebooks
Blue Sky: @ivymarie-author.bsky.social
X: @IvyMarie_Books
Website: www.ivymarieauthor.com

Don't forget about my wonderful cover artist - Shawna Russ;

Instagram: shawncolourart

Also By

Keep an eye out other books by Ivy Marie.

Contemporary Romance
Thief in Paris
Bad Decisions (Book 1 of Decisions Duet)
Late Decisions (Book 2 of Decisions Duet)
Surprised by Love ~ Coming 2025
Fan the Flames ~ Coming 2026

Paranormal Romance
Stolen Heart
His Hunter
Bound to the Reaper (Book 1 of Reaper)

Reaper Undercover (Book 2 of Reaper) ~ Coming 2026
Reaper Forever (Book 3 of Reaper) ~ Coming 2027
Witch Troubles ~ Coming 2025

Like Hell series (Paranormal Romance) ~ Coming 2028
Like Hell Mario (Prequel)
Like Hell this is Real (Book 1)
Like Hell this is Normal (Book 2)
Like Hell this is Happening (Book 3)
Like Hell Alternative (Alternate Reality)